Jake was in b

Not Jake, Christy
Not the boy you k
you don't know th

She felt his hand drift over her stomach, then slide up beneath the fullness of her breast. He squeezed gently, then plucked at the nipple with his fingers.

She tried not to respond even as she felt her body melt.

"Turn around," he whispered.

She couldn't say no. Gazing into his eyes, she knew that somewhere behind this stranger's hard, closed expression was the Jake she had once loved. She tensed as his hands moved lower. Hot colour flooded her face as she realized what her body was revealing to him.

Jake knew. He smiled. Eased her onto her back. Slid his body over hers. She almost started to cry—this was like so many mornings they'd spent together in Jake's apartment, beginning the day by making love.

But she couldn't really call *this* making love. It was more like making war...

To my friend, Janet Audick, for her kindness and compassionate heart (and George's spectacular soups!)

THE LAST SEDUCTION

BY

ELDA MINGER

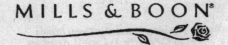

MILLS & BOON®

MILLS & BOON and MILLS & BOON with the Rose Device are registered trademarks of the publisher.
TEMPTATION is a registered trademark of Harlequin Enterprises Limited, used under licence.

First published in Great Britain 1997
by Harlequin Mills & Boon Limited,
Eton House, 18-24 Paradise Road, Richmond, Surrey TW9 1SR

© Elda Minger 1996

ISBN 0 263 80185 3

21-9702

Printed and bound in Great Britain
by BPC Paperbacks Limited, Aylesbury

Prologue

HE'D CONSCIOUSLY TRIED to forget her, but he'd never forgiven her.

The motorcycle sped over the San Bernardino Freeway, the driver isolated in the early-morning hours. At around 2 a.m., the desert landscape was still shrouded in darkness, and no sound but the relentless wind and the roar of the powerful Harley's engine disturbed Jake's thoughts as he headed toward Palm Springs.

He'd grown up in the desert community. Come into his own. Fallen in love. He'd never felt what he'd felt for Christy for any other woman. Twelve years after the fact, he still had trouble erasing her image from his mind, the sound of her voice, the soft scent of her skin that was hers alone.

It had been his idea to create the opportunity for this weird sort of exorcism. He wanted her out of his life, out of his soul, he wanted to finally be finished with her. And he didn't know any other way of doing it besides going to see her one last time, having it out with her.

Psychiatrists would have called what he was doing seeking closure; it wasn't his style. His thoughts were simpler: they bordered dangerously close to revenge. On simply taking a few days—a weekend at most—and burning her out of his memory.

She couldn't still have that singular, feminine power over him. She couldn't still arouse and excite him, overwhelm him, with just a look, a smile. It was only because of their background together, only because of what they'd been through together. Their past had formed an extremely close bond between them, something he'd believed could never be broken.

But it had not only been broken, it had been shattered. Irrevocably. Completely. She'd destroyed what they'd had, deliberately and consciously. She'd wanted out, and he'd seen that she got what she wanted. He'd driven to Los Angeles to seek fame and fortune, cursing the day he'd first seen her, first wanted her. First loved her.

But he'd never been able to forget her. Never. And now Jake found that he wanted to get on with his life—and he wanted her out of it. He wanted to sever any final ties he had to Christy, even if they were only in his own mind.

He gunned the engine on the powerful motorcycle, enjoying the Harley's sudden rush of power and speed. He'd set his plan in motion with utmost precision. He'd hired a private detective. He knew everything about Christy that the man had been able to ascertain. Where she lived, where she worked, what she did in her spare time.

He'd pieced together her life from the time he'd left, and a part of him had been pleased that she'd done so well.

That was the part he'd tried to eradicate. That was the part he wanted to put to rest. He couldn't afford to give her any mercy, none at all, if this long weekend was going to yield the results he wanted.

Hell, if he was completely honest with himself, he'd admit he'd never been able to forget or forgive her. But this weekend he was going to do both. His way. Whatever it took, he was going to stop thinking about Christy, he was going to take the ghosts of the past and put them firmly back where they belonged. He was going to get on with his life—without her.

He exited off the freeway onto Bob Hope Drive, slowing the powerful bike. As he drove into town, into Palm Desert where she worked, he began to recognize familiar sights. They gripped him with emotions he didn't want to feel as memories came rushing back.

All of them involving Christy.

He pulled off at a service station on the outskirts of town, gassed up the bike, grabbed a bottle of Coke and rechecked his directions to The Castaway, the bar where Christy worked.

He'd wait there until she showed up. He'd mapped out his life so that he had a week in which to put this straight, but hopefully it wouldn't take more than a weekend. He'd find her, follow her home and finish what had happened between them so long ago.

He wasn't going to hurt her, or threaten her. He just wanted a few answers after the fact. He wanted to know what had happened between them. He wanted one more glimpse of the old Christy, the honest Christy, the woman he'd loved.

He took one last slug of his Coke, then tossed the glass bottle into the trash. Mounting his motorcycle, Jake gunned the engine and headed into town.

Revenge is a dish best served cold, someone had once told him. Well, he was as cold as a man could get. His emotions had been encased in ice since Christy's betrayal, and it was about time he warmed them back up.

Revenge. He slowed the bike as he came up on the large resort hotel that sheltered the bar. There it was, in blue neon. A small neon palm tree, and the bold, slashing letters. The Castaway.

He smiled grimly as he parked his Harley at the far end of the lot. The Castaway. How ironic, when Christy had cast away anything they could've had together. As he walked toward the resort, he felt that familiar anger, that frustration over what she'd done to them, the utter incredulity of it, wash over him.

He stopped in the parking lot. Paused in his pursuit of her. The wind was still blowing, that restless desert wind he remembered so well. Jake took a few deep breaths of the dry, fragrant air and centered himself. He could do this. He had to do this. He had to get her out of his heart and out of his soul because he had to get on with his life.

At nineteen, he'd been destroyed by what she'd done to him. To them. Twelve years later, at thirty-one, he was in his prime. A mature man. Surely he was capable of forgiveness and understanding. Surely she would consent to sit with him for a small amount of time.

Maybe it would all be over the moment he saw her. Maybe he'd take one look at her and feel . . . nothing. Perhaps that would be all it would take, and he wouldn't even have to talk to her.

He continued across the parking lot, toward the resort bar. Rock music, the beat loud and insistent, could be heard, along with the sounds of laughter. Though it was only a Thursday night, it was the first night in a long, three-day weekend. Memorial Day. Ironic.

He walked inside the bar.

1

SHE THOUGHT SHE SAW HIM.

Christy Garrett paused while wiping down the bar and stared into the dense crowd. She was tired. For a moment, she thought she'd seen Jake McCrae.

Jake. She couldn't quite control the well of emotion that came surging to the surface at the thought of him. Even after twelve years, the man's memory did more to her emotions than most of the flesh-and-blood specimens that paraded through The Castaway night after night.

She'd gotten over Jake. Hadn't she?

"Christy. Go home."

She started at the sound of her friend's voice. Keith, the other bartender and part owner, was a teddy bear of a man and one of her very best friends. He listened to everyone's problems as he mixed them drinks. He'd listened to quite a few of her own.

"I should." She smiled, relieved to put the memory of Jake out of her mind. Anyone could put the power of their memories in perspective, and she could as well. She thought of him once in a while, thought of what could've been. Bittersweet memories. Better left alone. There had been a dark-haired man in a distant corner who'd looked like Jake. That was all. It would've sparked a memory in anyone.

"I can't talk you into coming over for the big bash?" Keith said, teasing her affectionately. He was like the big brother she'd never had. The big brother Jake could've never been.

Jake. Put him out of your mind.

"Nope. I have a long weekend of total solitude coming my way, and I'm looking forward to it." She reached up and gently tugged on a lock of his brown hair. He wore it long, and she knew he liked the gesture.

"I can't tempt you? Volleyball? Ribs? Hamburgers on the grill?"

She sighed, then laughed. "It sounds wonderful, but I need a little time to myself. Maybe I'll come by late Sunday night."

Keith laughed. "We'll still be partying."

His parties were infamous around the desert community. Anyone was invited. It wasn't unlike Keith to round up the last few customers in the bar and take them to his place for an impromptu movie-fest on his VCR and big-screen TV. His energy and joy in living was contagious, and he'd talked her out of many a blue mood.

"You've been working too hard. You need to play."

She shook her head. "I'm going up to Rutger's house to sit in his hot tub. Then I'm going to sleep in tomorrow, get some sun, cook up a little gourmet food and ponder the mysteries of life."

Keith frowned. "Then even the thought of my potato salad can't tempt you?"

"Nope." She softened her rejection with a smile. "It's not you, Keith. You know that."

"I know." He scanned the bar, gave a customer a refill on her Coke, then continued the conversation. "Just don't get lost in your memories, Christy. I don't like to see you so sad."

She felt the smile on her face falter. Sometimes Keith was just too damn perceptive.

She needed this long weekend alone. She planned on resting, lying out in the sun and figuring out what she was going to do with the rest of her life. She was twenty-nine, just on the edge of turning thirty, and she had to make some crucial decisions. Specifically, what to do with Arthur.

Arthur Beck—Art, as he liked to be called—was a very nice man. An engineer. And that was about it. She'd met him through her business, they'd become friends and he'd been quite clear that he wanted their relationship to deepen. She knew if she married him she would have a quiet, secure life. She thought she wanted that, after all she'd been through.

But somehow, as the time for her decision came closer and closer, she still wasn't sure.

Rutger Huss had given her just the chance she needed this weekend. She knew the world famous artist through her business, Mom Cat, an in-home pet-sitting service. He had three felines of his own, and didn't particularly want to take them to Paris with him during the next three weeks. She'd agreed, as was usual with her customers, to stay in his huge modern house in the cool hills above the desert floor and take care of everything.

If she did a little gardening while she house-sat, that was all right. If she watered a few plants or made sure a sofa was delivered, it was all part of the job. But her main duty was to make sure the cats in question didn't have their routine upset, their lives disturbed. Cats were sensitive creatures; they usually liked their lives just the way they were.

Rutger's cats were easy, all three of them. Since she was going to be up there for so long, he'd told her to go ahead and bring her own cat to his home, as well. Sparky got along with just about everyone, so she wasn't worried about cat fights.

But the main reason she'd delighted in taking the job was the isolation of Rutger's huge house. No one would be there, and only Keith had the phone number—with instructions not to call this entire weekend. She needed the solitude, needed the time alone to figure out what she was going to tell this very nice man.

Nice. She frowned. Since when had nice not been good enough?

Since Jake, she thought, then pushed his memory out of her mind. Or tried to.

It was incredible. She'd loved Jake since she turned sixteen. She'd looked up to him, admired him, hadn't been able to believe her good fortune in having him in

her life. He'd been unlike anyone she'd ever known.
She'd treasured their relationship, known exactly how
special it was—and then turned around and deliberately destroyed it.

Christy smiled at a customer and made him a Long
Island Iced Tea. She wiped down the counter once
again, listened to a few more jokes and all the time
counted the minutes until she could leave.

She knew Keith meant well, telling her she could
leave, but she couldn't let him deal with a crowd like
this alone. The bar was packed, people were ready to
party, everyone wanted to kick off this particular
Memorial Day weekend with a vengeance. So she
talked and laughed with the regulars, mixed drinks,
refilled bowls of peanuts and pretzels and generally
made herself quite useful until closing time at around
three in the morning.

Walking out to the parking lot, she shivered as the
desert wind touched her. For just an instant she closed
her eyes and wished things could have been different. . . .

"One last chance," Keith teased, unlocking the door
to his red Jeep Cherokee.

"Nope." She walked over toward his car, glad of the
chance to escape her own morbid thoughts. It was just
about the same time of year she'd broken things off
with Jake. This was the weekend, she suddenly decided, to get him out of her memories once and for all.

"Sure?"

"Yep." She wagged a finger at him with mock sternness. "And don't try to call me and tempt me, because I won't be picking up the phone. Rutger's machine will be on and the ringer will be turned off." She paused, wondering if she should even reveal the next fact, then suddenly needed the reassurance of a close friend. "I'm giving Arthur his answer next Wednesday, when I see him for dinner."

She saw Keith's hesitation, then his frown, before he answered.

"Ah, Christy. . ." He hesitated, and she knew what he was going to say.

"Just say it."

"You're sure that's what you want?"

"I don't know. But I have to make some kind of decision. I can't just keep going on the way I am, drifting, tending bar and looking after other people's cats. I want. . ." Her voice faltered. There had been so many things she'd wanted, dreams she'd shared with Jake, so many hopes. . . . Why was his image so persistent in her mind?

The man in the bar.

The time of year.

The thought of marriage—to another man, when she'd only ever really belonged to Jake.

She was tired. That was it. She was tired, and when she got this way, it made it easier for old memories to surface. To intrude.

"I want . . . a lot more than I've got."

"I know." He put his arm around her shoulders and gave her a brief hug. "And you deserve a lot more."

She rested her forehead against his shirtfront, enjoying the simple human contact. Keith had been a good friend to her through the years, and for just a moment she wondered what life would've been like if there had been that incredible, indefinable chemistry between them.

"I should marry you." She laughed, the sound muffled against his shirt.

He started to laugh then, as well. It was a fact in their desert community that Keith treasured his bachelor status. Christy often teased him, saying she couldn't wait for him to meet the right woman. The bigger they were, the harder they fell.

"I think I would marry you, before I'd let you spend the rest of your life with old Arthur."

"He's not old—"

"He's barely thirty-five and he'd old, Christy. He's an old man in a young man's body."

She stepped back from him then, not wanting to hear it, not wanting to face what she knew was a deep truth.

"Keith."

The look of resignation on his face told her he knew he'd gone too far.

"Don't make any decisions you can't undo, Christy."

"But I have to do something!"

"No, you don't. Take the weekend. Rest. Get some sun, take care of yourself. I'll see you at work on Tuesday night, and you let me know what you've decided." He grinned then, his smile rakish. "And if it's Old Man Beck, I'll talk you out of it."

"But I can't—"

"Someone will come along. Someone perfect. But not Beck, Christy. Contentment is for cows."

"And what's that supposed to mean?"

"Just what it sounds like. You'd be bored stiff within a month, and you know it."

She didn't like the direction this conversation was heading, it was forcing her to look too close to home.

"Arthur is—"

"A very nice man. I know. He is. And he needs a very nice girl."

The outraged look she gave him made him start to laugh as he unlocked the driver's side door of his Jeep.

"Not that you're not nice. You're very nice. You're just too much for our Mr. Beck. You need someone . . . stronger."

Jake. His image came to mind, and she pushed it aside. Jake was in Los Angeles, tending to his career. Jake the daredevil. Jake the actor. Jake, who she both never wanted to see again and was sometimes so lonely for she wondered if she'd ever have any emotion left over for another man.

"I'll see you Tuesday night," she called, backing away from his Jeep and toward her Thunderbird. "And don't call."

"I won't. But call me if you need to talk. Anytime."

She unlocked the door to her car and slid inside, thankful to be out of the wind. Once inside, she watched as Keith's Jeep made its way out of the parking lot. Palm trees bent against the wind as she saw his turn signal blink red, then the Jeep headed left and disappeared.

What did she want? She didn't have a clue.

Not wanting to think too deeply, she started her car and began the journey to Rutger's house.

THE HOUSE was completely modern—all white walls and huge glass windows, with lots of exotic cacti in every available area. Some of them were in bloom now, their flowers vivid and exotically dark against the gleaming white walls.

A full moon brought everything into sharp relief as Christy pulled into the driveway and pressed the button on her garage door opener that would open the massive gates. They slid open and she drove inside.

Rutger cherished his privacy. He was a flamboyant presence in the art world, and made headlines often as the bad boy of his profession. But the reality was that he was rather sweet, and spent long periods of time alone with just his cats for company as he painted his remarkable canvases.

She'd met him at the vet's when they'd struck up a conversation. He'd liked the fact that she didn't know who he was. Once he'd found out what she did for a living, he'd hired her on the spot. He was out of town a lot, he said, and his cats got upset. He'd been at the vet's for a behavioral consultation, as Sasha was slowly destroying one of the white leather living-room sofas.

The vet had recommended that Christy baby-sit the temperamental little Siamese. Sasha was lonely without anyone in the house. She needed more than the company of the housekeeper, who usually kept to her own rooms when she didn't pop in twice a day to feed the feline brood.

She needed love and reassurance, and that was Christy's specialty.

Rutger didn't know anything about the mess her own life was currently in, or how special the use of his house was for this particular weekend. Christy made a practice of not mixing her personal life and Mom Cat. She tried not to let one influence the other.

As she stared at the huge white house, glowing beneath a desert moon, she wondered at how far she'd come. If she closed her eyes, she could see her father in their tiny apartment, snoring in his recliner. The television would have been on, as always. Probably tuned to a game show or an old Western.

She'd wanted more, and she'd overcome the guilt that simple desire had inspired a long time ago.

She got out of the car, grabbing her purse and locking the door. For just a moment, she paused. The desert came alive at night, especially a night like this, all wild and windy, with just a hint of chill in the air. There was something completely primal about the feel of the wind off the desert, and it spoke to something deep in her soul.

Jake would've loved it.

She didn't stop to reflect long. There were four hungry cats inside, she'd worked a double shift and hadn't had time to come home and feed them. Rutger's housekeeper had the long weekend off; she'd gone to Riverside to see her daughter and four grandchildren.

The feline tribe that waited for her inside the door would be demanding and noisy as she entered the house, and at the moment she welcomed their furry company.

HE WATCHED HER enter the huge white house and was thankful she was alone. The thought of her with another man, especially a man like Rutger Huss, was too much to bear.

He'd followed her to Rutger's house, carefully. Far enough behind her Thunderbird that she hadn't a clue. Jake felt slightly guilty stalking her in such a manner, but as he didn't intend her any harm, he forced the emotion down.

Getting onto the grounds was easy enough. He'd left his bike parked in a safe place, and climbing a wall was no big deal. Getting inside the house might be a problem, especially if the alarm system was elaborate.

But even if he set it off, he had a feeling Christy wouldn't turn him in. Not if he explained what it was he wanted to do. And that part still wasn't clear, even in his own mind.

Just talk? He wasn't sure anymore. The flood of emotions that had been released when he'd first seen her had shocked him. It had been as if twelve years had simply fallen away, as if the time that had passed didn't even matter. He still wanted her. He might not love her, but he still wanted her with a hunger that had shaken him to the core.

He'd watched her from the parking lot as she'd talked to her friend. Keith Tenney, the detective had said. Keith, the perennial good-time guy and happy bachelor. He hadn't been surprised at the flash of jealousy and possessiveness that had overtaken him when he'd seen the bartender put his arm around Christy's slender shoulders.

Some feelings weren't meant to change, and his own for Christy were in that category.

He watched as lights went on in the large, modern house. He waited a few minutes, then headed in that direction.

SHE'D KICKED OFF her high heels and disposed of her panty hose. The cool tile kitchen floor felt like heaven against her bare feet. The cats were fed, and she thought about curling up with a good book and distracting herself. Just for tonight. She'd think about her life, her problems, in the morning. Right now, she was tired.

Maybe a hot bath and bed. That sounded appealing. Christy leaned her elbows on the kitchen counter and watched as the cats made short work of the cans she'd opened and the contents she'd placed in their pottery bowls on the gleaming white floor.

She glanced outside, at the turquoise expanse of water that filled the large, Olympic-size pool. It had been one of the reasons Rutger had bought the house, or so he'd told her. He was a big man, and needed his exercise. Hours of concentration at his easels tended to cause his shoulders and neck muscles to stiffen, and swimming was an excellent preventive measure.

A swim. Perfect. She reached down absently and patted Sparky's head as she ate. The chubby calico looked up for just a second, appreciative of the attention, then concentrated on the smelly fish in her bowl.

She hadn't brought a swimsuit. She was alone, after all. And though it wasn't always wise to swim alone, she would be extremely careful. Just a short dip. Just enough movement through that soothing, cool turquoise water to get some of the stiffness out of her shoulders. Just enough to calm her nerves.

She stepped out the French doors that led from the kitchen to the patio, then started down the tiled steps toward the pool.

HE'D SKIRTED the main house easily, and had been in the shelter of a huge hibiscus bush when he saw her start down toward the pool. Not wanting to frighten her, he stepped deeper into the shadows.

A swim? He'd let her take a swim, then follow her into the house and confront her. Perhaps the strongest element he had in his favor was the element of surprise. She didn't expect to see him, he was certain of that. They hadn't spoken at all since their breakup twelve years ago.

He wondered if she would think he was strange, needing to come to see her one more time, needing this chance to get on with his life. And he didn't care. Jake had often followed his instincts, and they'd never let him down. His gut told him he needed this quiet interlude, the answers to questions he'd speculated on for far too long.

It was time for answers, and Christy was the only person who could give them to him.

He almost stepped out of the shadows, almost called her name. Then she skimmed the ribbed black tank top over her head and let it fall to the tiled floor, and his mouth went dry.

She was still beautiful. Christy had possessed a body that, even at the age of sixteen, had driven men wild. It had gotten her into trouble more often than she'd wanted to admit, and had even precipitated the way they'd met. She'd always appeared more mature than her actual age. Now, as he looked at her, she slid out of her short black skirt and stood beside the pool in only her bra and panties.

A noise from the kitchen caught her attention and she turned toward the house. "No roughhousing, guys!" He assumed she was talking to Rutger's cats.

He'd also assumed that the scrap of black lace she'd been wearing was a pair of panties, but now realized it was the briefest of G-strings.

The blood started pounding heavily in his veins. Absolute masculine rage at the idea of Rutger Huss touching her caused any sensible thoughts he'd even briefly possessed to vanish.

He started forward, out of the concealment of the lushly landscaped foliage, and checked himself just in time.

Rutger wasn't here. He knew that. He also knew that Christy's business, Mom Cat, was successful because of the personal attention she gave to all her clients. Just because she was taking care of Rutger's cats, Jake knew he didn't have to make the very illogical leap of thought and assume she was taking care of Rutger's sexual needs.

She unhooked her bra, and the wisp of black lace floated to the ground. He closed his eyes and groaned softly. Things were rapidly escalating out of control. He'd thought if he could come out to the desert to see her, they could talk like two rational adults.

Instead he'd seen her in the bar and it had started all over again. That instantaneous, painful wanting. That indefinable attraction, so strong that twelve years apart hadn't made the slightest difference. The knowledge that she hadn't wanted him, hadn't ever wanted him. The pain. And the shame.

The rage.

She skimmed the G-string over her slim hips, then walked to the far edge of the Olympic-size pool and dived in.

He watched her swim, watched the natural, unselfconscious way she moved her body. Christy had been a virgin when they'd met, but she'd delighted in her body, in the feelings he'd evoked, in their mutual pleasure. He'd loved her, treasured their time together, would've done anything for her.

Now he simply watched. And waited.

She didn't swim long. Within fifteen minutes, she was climbing up the ladder at the deep end, then walking down the long side of the large pool, closer, closer . . .

She passed within inches of his hiding place, and he simply, finally reacted. Without thinking through the consequences, without caring, he reached out and grabbed her arm.

She whirled, shock and outrage sparking her eyes, then the quickest, most violent of recognitions. But she recovered admirably, and didn't struggle.

"Jake," she said quietly. But he could see the pulse pounding rapidly in her throat, and knew she wasn't as composed as she appeared to be.

He nodded his head, unable to speak.

They stood that way for a long moment, then she moved away from him. He tightened his grip on her arm, and she flashed him a look of—what? Anger? Annoyance? Despair?

"Let me go," she said quietly, and he couldn't figure out the tone of her voice. He knew, at that exact moment, that he'd bungled things badly, that this whole scenario couldn't get much worse. He didn't really know what to do.

Then instinct took over.

He stepped closer. Threaded the fingers of his other hand through her wet, pale blond hair, angled her head toward his, touched his lips to hers—and kissed her.

It all came flooding back, and in that instant he knew he had to have her, had to be close to her, lie next to her, be inside her, one last time.

She must have sensed the change when he drew back. Christy looked up at him, her green eyes wide, her lips trembling. She tried to pull away from him, but he held firm.

"I can't let you go," he whispered.

2

Fourteen years ago . . .

SHE KNEW what Rick wanted, but she wasn't going to make it easy for him.

"Damn it, Christy, stop fighting me! You know you want it."

"Stop it—*no!*" She was struggling wildly in the back seat of the car, not caring what he thought, only knowing she had to get out of the Chevy Impala.

"Come on, baby, I know—*ow!*" Rick's eyes narrowed with anger as he looked down at her. She'd managed to clumsily elbow him, and now for the first time this evening Christy was truly afraid.

"You little bitch. You led me on, and now you're telling me to stop?"

She made an ineffectual grab for her top before he pinned her hands above her head. Then, with his other hand, he grabbed the front of her bra and pulled down. Hard.

It gave, she could hear the sharp ripping sound. She was naked from the waist up. Tears of anger and humiliation filled her eyes as she continued to struggle.

What happened next was so fast it seemed like a blur. The back passenger door opened, then Rick was grabbed by the collar of his open denim shirt. He was pulled out from the back seat so quickly Christy didn't even have a chance to see who her rescuer was.

"She said no," a deep voice informed Rick. And Rick, being a typical bully when faced with a fair fight, began to whimper and whine.

"She was having fun—"

"It didn't sound like she was having fun to me."

"What the hell business is it of yours, any—"

"Shut up. Just shut up and let her out of the car."

"Hey man, screw you! You don't know what was going down—"

A scuffle ensued as Christy reached for her mangled top. The raspberry-colored cotton sweater had torn, and was just about unwearable. She adjusted her white, lacy bra, but the front fastening had broken and it didn't hold together. Not caring what she looked like, only knowing she had to get away from this whole scene, she slipped the torn sweater over her head so the undamaged side covered her front. Grabbing her small gray canvas duffel bag, she slipped out of the car just in time to see the stranger deck Rick.

Rick registered the oddest look of surprise before he slid down the side of the car, landing with a satisfying thump on his butt in the dust.

She was walking swiftly away from the car when the stranger caught up with her.

"Here." He'd taken off his shirt and was handing it to her. She stopped in her tracks, looking up at him. And she had to look up. She'd seen him before, in school. He was a year ahead of her, a junior to her sophomore status. She didn't know how she'd ever face him Monday in school. Or Rick, for that matter.

She didn't even know this stranger's name.

"Put it on."

She glanced away from him, quickly weighing her options, hating to be in debt to him. But she couldn't realistically walk home in a torn sweater with her bra hanging open. Not that her father would notice. But that wasn't the problem. Getting home safely was.

"Thanks." She reached for the shirt and put it on. It was black cotton, and still warm from his body. It smelled like him, and that made her uneasy as she quickly buttoned the garment.

"Need a ride?"

He must have interpreted the expression on her face at the thought of getting in a car with another man, because he said shortly, "I'm not going to maul you. I just want to make sure you get home safely."

"Why should you care?" she snapped back. Her experience with the world had taught her that no one gave anyone anything for free. Not without wanting something in return. And the last thing she wanted was another so-called relationship.

She'd thought Rick liked her. Really liked her. Wanted something like a relationship. What a little fool she'd been. What had happened tonight told her he wanted only one thing from her—just like all the others.

"I don't treat women the way Rick does."

And somehow, she knew he didn't. Call it instinct, female intuition, or whatever, but as she stood at one of the far back corners of the Circle K parking lot, she knew she had nothing to fear from this man.

"All right. But just a ride."

"Fine."

They drove in silence along Palm Canyon Drive. She didn't look at him, but was somehow always conscious of his presence. She felt safe in his car, a Mustang that had seen better days. But it ran, and it was safe, and that was all she was concerned with at the moment.

She turned in her seat, indignant, when he pulled into the Denny's parking lot.

"I thought you said—"

"You've got a bruise on your cheek. I thought you might like a chance to clean up before having to explain it all to your folks." He reached in the back seat, grabbed a black T-shirt and pulled it on.

It was on the tip of her tongue to tell him her father wouldn't give a damn and her mother had been dead for years. But it wasn't the sort of confession one made to a perfect stranger. A rather considerate stranger.

She hesitated, suddenly feeling ashamed of her swift assessment of his motives. "Thanks."

"I'll get some coffee while you clean up."

He seemed to have everything under control. She envied him that quality. Her life seemed to be spinning out of control. She didn't even want to think about what might have happened if this stranger hadn't helped her.

"Jake, right?" She guessed at his name. Their high school was small, and she had kind of noticed him when he'd transferred in.

He smiled as they walked toward the all-night restaurant. "Got it in one. Christy?"

She was inexplicably glad he knew her name. "Yeah."

They parted at the entrance, she for the ladies room, he for a booth. She didn't intend to join him for coffee—or anything.

CHRISTY barely made it to the bathroom before reaction took over. Several teenage girls were crowded around the large mirror over the double sink, gossiping and laughing, so she lowered her head, letting her long blond hair cover her face as she darted into one of the far stalls. Flipping the lid down, she sat, wrapping her arms around her upper body as she began to shake.

They hadn't seen her. Hadn't seen the bruise, or her disheveled appearance.

If there was one thing Christy was a master at, it was deceiving people. Most didn't look too closely anyway, or only saw what they wanted to see.

As she sat, shaking, another girl entered the large public bathroom.

"You'll never guess who's here!"

"Who?"

"Jake McCrae!"

"God, he's so gorgeous—"

"Who's he going out with?"

"I don't know, but I'd like to get in line!"

More laughter, then, "Did you know Rick Friedman is dating Christy Garrett?"

She heard a snort of laughter, then one girl said, "If you can call that dating."

Laughter all around, as Christy held her breath, wishing she were anywhere on Earth but in this particular bathroom.

"She's such a slut."

"I know! There's only one reason he'd want to date her!" The voice paused. "I think he's kind of cute."

"But not as cute as Jake," another voice quickly amended.

"No way! Jake's in a class all by himself."

Tears stung Christy's eyes, but she held back her anger. No one knew what she was really like—no one. She was damned if she would break down in front of these caustic bitches.

The light in the bathroom was such that she could see the bruise on her upper left cheekbone. Taking compact foundation out of her bag, she carefully covered the dark ugly color. Then she quickly repaired her eye makeup, brushed her hair, then stripped off Jake's shirt.

She'd been wearing her torn sweater and bra when he'd given her his shirt, and had buttoned the garment over them. Now she took off her damaged clothing and stuffed it into her duffel, then rebuttoned the shirt. Instead of buttoning it all the way down, she tied it beneath her breasts. Her stomach was flat and firm, and her short skirt had escaped unscathed.

She looked fine.

Christy waited until the last of the gossips left the bathroom, then she vacated the stall. Stopping for a quick check in the mirror and satisfied she looked as good as possible, she exited the bathroom with an entirely new battle plan in mind.

The girls who had been gossiping about her were here after a movie—girls' night out. They'd probably ordered something, as the one all-night restaurant in town was something of a hangout for the high school.

It wouldn't hurt for them to see her with Jake.

And it would counteract anything Rick would be tempted to say about her. It would look like sour grapes on his part.

Screw them all, she thought as she walked toward the booth Jake was occupying. Just as she'd thought, three of the girls from the little bathroom gabfest were crowded around his booth.

"Hi, Jake. Sorry I'm so late." Christy slid into the booth, then smiled up at her three classmates, enjoying herself immensely. She'd injected just the right amount of intimacy into her tone, making it sound as if she and Jake were much closer than they actually were. Who had to know they'd really just met tonight?

Her status would rise, even if they all believed she was sleeping with everyone and anyone. Having sex with Jake was a huge step up from Rick, and she knew it. She also wanted to make them jealous and frustrated, wanted them to know what it felt like to feel as if they didn't belong, and could never get what they wanted.

Their expressions were priceless. First incredulity, then flushed cheeks, then quickly mumbled excuses. Finally a swift exit toward their large booth in the corner.

Christy settled into her side of the booth, slinging her bag on the inside of her seat.

"Thanks," she said softly. She owed him that much.

He merely nodded his head. She watched, fascinated, as a smile played around the corners of his expressive mouth.

"What?"

"That shirt looks a hell of a lot better on you than it ever did on me."

She could feel her cheeks warming in response to his compliment. Somehow, and she didn't know why, when Jake made a remark about how she looked, it didn't sound . . . sleazy.

She could feel the eyes of her classmates on the two of them. Wondering. Speculating. Trying to figure the whole thing out. Which would probably take them a while, because she still hadn't figured it out.

"Did you order your coffee?" She asked it more because she didn't know what else to say. He made her nervous, but not the same way Rick had. She didn't feel afraid of him. Just . . . nervous.

"I waited for you." He picked up one of the plastic-coated menus and opened it. "I was thinking about a piece of chocolate cream pie. You want something?"

This was heading dangerously close to an actual date. But it was nice. It had been a long time since a guy had treated her with this much respect. But Jake was new to town, and he didn't know the score. She was sure that, come Monday at school, someone in one of his classes or in the hallway during a break would give him the news.

In a moment of uncharacteristic boldness, she decided to do it herself. No use letting a nice guy think he was going out with a nice girl.

"You know about . . . you know about me, don't you?" She hated asking the question, but it had to be done.

"Know what?" His eyes never left the menu.

"About . . . my reputation."

That got his attention. He glanced up at her, and their gazes locked. For a moment, she couldn't draw breath. He had the bluest eyes she'd ever seen. The exact color of Glass Plus. She almost laughed at the thought, comparing a guy's eyes to a cleaner, but it was true.

True, true, clear and blue. He studied her for a long moment, until she almost squirmed against the vinyl seat.

"I make up my own mind."

"Oh."

"About just about everything."

"Oh."

"I waited for you." He picked up one of the coated means and

"You got a problem with that?"

She swallowed, her throat suddenly dry and tight. "No."

"Good."

Their waiter arrived, he ordered a cup of coffee and a slice of chocolate cream pie. She was so flustered, she did the same. She'd completely forgotten about any audience they might have and concentrated on the man sitting across from her.

That was the difference. Rick and his cronies were boys. Jake might have been the same biological age, but he was clearly a man. A mature man. She smiled suddenly, glad he chose to take no part in the gossip that was part and parcel of high school life.

"What's so funny?"

"You," she said boldly. "You're different."

He grinned then, and she had a feeling he'd heard this more than once. "I have no trouble with that."

They talked for almost three hours. He asked her all sorts of questions, questions no one had ever bothered to ask her before.

"What do you want to do?"

"What do you mean?" She'd just swallowed the last of her fourth cup of coffee, and knew she'd be up all night after all this caffeine. The thought didn't bother her a bit. He fascinated her; he was unlike any man she'd ever known.

"After you finish school."

She'd never thought about it. Well, maybe she had. Secretly she'd hoped for a man to come take her away from the confusion and depression of her father's life. Take her away and protect her. Love her. Cherish her.

"I haven't given it a lot of thought."

He stared at her, as if trying to see inside her mind, and it made her nervous.

"Don't do it."

"What?"

"Stare at me like that. Like—"

"Like trying to see inside your brain?"

"That's it exactly."

"Sorry. Bad habit." He drained the last of his coffee and set the mug down. "I just really like to get to the bottom of things."

"I can see that."

The girls from the bathroom had long gone by the time they walked back out to his car.

"I'll get the shirt to you on Monday. If you want to meet me out in the parking lot—"

"I'll find you. We'll connect in the hallway between classes."

"But if they see me giving you your shirt, they'll think—"

"I don't really give a damn what they think."

She stared up at him as he unlocked the passenger door for her and knew he was telling the truth. And she admired him for it. Jake McCrae apparently made up his own mind about things.

They were almost to her apartment when she thought of him walking her to the door and seeing how she lived. Jake was the kind of guy who saw a woman home.

She couldn't allow it.

"You can just drop me off at the next corner," she hedged, suddenly nervous. She didn't want him to meet her father. Not now, maybe not ever.

"No way. I'm taking you home." He softened his words with a smile. "No telling what kind of trouble you might get into if I don't."

She laughed at that, surprising herself. He was funny and kind, and both those qualities meant more to her than if he'd been drop-dead handsome—which he was.

"I can't talk you out of it?"

"No."

She gave him directions, and soon he pulled up in front of the shabby apartment complex she called home.

"I'm on the first floor . . . it's just to the left of the walkway, you don't have to—"

He was already getting out of the car.

"If you want me to talk to your father, I will. I didn't realize we were going to be out this late. He should know about what you went through tonight."

As if he could cope with it. "No, it's all right. He'll be asleep, I don't want to wake him up. He's been kind of ill—"

Drunk, you mean.

She was thankful Jake didn't push it. "Okay."

He saw her to her doorstep, but didn't make a move to kiss her. Instead he waited until she unlocked the door and stepped inside the dark apartment, illuminated only by the flickering glow from the small television on the far side of the boxy living room.

"Thanks, Jake. I . . . I appreciate what you did for me."

"No problem. See you in school on Monday?"

"Yeah—I'll get the shirt to you."

"That's not what I meant."

She knew what he meant, and she almost couldn't allow herself to believe it. She smiled up at him, wondering if her dream had a chance of coming true after all.

"Okay," she whispered.

"I'll see you on Monday," he said again, then backed off the front step, still looking at her.

She'd almost closed the front door when she heard his voice. Even though he whispered, it carried perfectly on the still, spring desert air.

"Christy? I had a great time tonight."

HER FATHER was asleep in his reclining chair when she walked into the living room. She'd put a screen up by the front door, so that the living room was afforded a little more privacy than it would have normally had.

A movie channel was on, the sound turned low. Her father had nodded off and a lit cigarette was in his hand. It had barely burned down, and she figured he hadn't been asleep long. She took it out of his hand, stubbed it out, covered him with one of the afghans on the couch and turned off the television.

Upstairs, she undressed, threw away both her ruined sweater and bra, then stripped off her clothes, changed into her nightgown and padded into the bathroom.

She took a good look at herself and wondered why Jake would want to spend time with her. The face that stared back at her had had too much makeup on even before she'd attempted to cover up that bruise. Dark black lines ringed her eyes, a slash of vivid blush graced each cheekbone. Her lip gloss was shiny and obvious, her nails long and dark with polish.

She studied her face for a long moment, then started the water running and rubbed her facial soap over her hands, working up a lather. She scrubbed her face until it stung, then rinsed and rinsed and rinsed.

Monday would be different. *She* would be different. Maybe she could start all over with Jake, have the chance at a different sort of relationship. Maybe if he really did think for himself, he'd listen to her when she told him the truth. . . .

Once in bed upstairs, she couldn't stop thinking about the evening. Meeting Jake had completely wiped the ugly incident with Rick out of her mind. She was still full of Jake, the way he looked, the way he smiled, even the way he ate his pie.

The sun was just coming up as she started to fall asleep. Before she gave in to the impulse, she changed into his shirt, then climbed beneath the covers to dream about him.

MONDAY was a revelation.

Rick never said a word to anyone. She found out almost a year later that Jake had met him before first period and told him what he would do to him if he even hinted at anything. Rick, typically, had caved in.

Jake was waiting for her outside her first class, English Composition, and she walked right up to him, completely at ease. Or as at ease as a girl could be when her heart was pounding a hundred beats a second.

"I brought your shirt," she began, not knowing what to say.

"Thanks." He seemed preoccupied. On edge. "What are you doing for lunch?"

She wondered what he was worried about. "Nothing."

"Want to leave and go get a burger?"

"Sure." She felt the tension leave his body, and suddenly realized he'd been worried about her reaction. The thought astounded her. "I'd like that," she added, wanting to reassure him.

"Okay. I'll meet you back in the parking lot at noon."

The day dragged interminably after that. All she could think about was lunch with Jake, and perhaps they could talk after school. She wanted to be with him; she didn't want to think any further than that.

When the noon bell rang, she was out of her seat in a flash, dumped her textbooks into her locker, grabbed her duffel and was out the door.

He was waiting for her, his Mustang looking reassuringly familiar.

"Taco House okay? They have great burgers."

She threw her bag into the back seat and climbed in the front, knowing many of their classmates were watching them. Speculating. Whatever hadn't been discussed over the weekend would be discussed over the phone tonight.

"Sounds great." She thought about trying for a blasé attitude, playing hard to get. She couldn't. She felt like a puppy that wanted to be loved, bouncing all over the car seat. Though she sat quietly, her heart wouldn't stop racing.

This was going to be different. She could feel it.

"What's in that bag?" he asked as he steered the car out of the school parking lot.

"My life," she said simply. The considering look he shot her didn't go unnoticed. With a sudden flash of intuition, of feminine insight, she knew she'd be able to eventually tell Jake everything.

He'd get it. He would understand.

3

Thursday evening, Memorial Day weekend

CHRISTY SWAM the length of Rutger's huge pool, then floated on her back and gazed up at the sky. Out in the desert where the air was so clear, the stars were so bright you had the feeling you could reach up and pluck one out of the night sky.

I wish ... I wish ...

Her wishes always took her back to Jake. Funny how you could remember someone so clearly. She'd thought she and Jake were soul mates. She'd let him get closer to her than anyone. Christy closed her eyes, trying to force back the sudden surge of emotion.

Twelve years ago ...

Twelve years ago, this weekend, she'd done what she'd thought was right. She'd sent Jake out of her life in the most horrible way possible. She'd wanted to make sure he would never come back, that his dreams would never die because of having to take care of her.

She'd thought of him every day since then. Wondered if he was safe. Secure. Loved. Sometimes she allowed herself the thought, what if, but usually it brought too much pain. She kept her emotions under control, but she'd learned to do that a long time ago.

She continued to float in the pool, feeling as if she were alone in the world, the last person on earth, floating along in the cool depths.

You're tired. And you saw a man who looked like Jake. That's all....

She didn't pursue this line of thought, because deep in her heart she knew it wasn't true. She knew if she married Arthur she would be giving him a mere shadow of what she was. And was that fair? He would get what he desired, he'd already told her he wanted to marry her. Even in the face of her obvious hesitation, he'd assured her that he loved her enough for both of them.

But was it right? She had no illusions about why she would finally marry Arthur. She was lonely. Deeply, completely, throughout the body all the way to your bones lonely. She was at a crossroads of her life, almost turning thirty. She'd put her life in a sort of emotional deep freeze since ending her relationship with Jake, and now wanted—had to—make the decision to keep going. To build some sort of a life for herself.

She wanted marriage. And children. If not Jake's—

Even through her closed eyes, a tear managed to slip out. This was far more painful than she'd thought. Christy had consciously decided that she needed this long weekend alone to think, to go deep within herself, to consider what she wanted to do with the rest of her life. She could have ignored it, could have gone to Keith's bash and flitted from group to group, laughed, pushed down the deeper, more emotional thoughts that had a way of cropping up at odd moments.

But she'd decided to face it head-on. And it was incredibly painful, far more than she would have expected, given the years that had passed since her breakup with Jake.

You have to say goodbye....

She swam to the far end of the pool, then climbed out, using the metal ladder. The desert night air was cool, and she shivered in reaction. She'd forgotten a towel, but it wasn't far to the door, and the kitchen was warm.

She walked along the side of the pool, then almost jumped out of her skin when a hand closed over her arm.

She whirled, fear and adrenaline rushing through her, ready to fight, then within seconds her shocked senses recognized Jake.

Jake. The tiled walkway beside the pool seemed to rock beneath her feet as she stared at him. It had to have only been seconds, but the moment lengthened, expanded, to take in all reaction, sensation.

"Jake," she said quietly. She had the almost painful, irresistible urge to sway toward him, to let him take her in his arms. It horrified her to realize that nothing mattered, not the years, not the pain, not the anger and despair. She wanted to be with him, next to him, close to him. Her body responded before any rational thought had a chance to block its responses.

He merely nodded his head. She couldn't tell what he was thinking, there was an enigmatic darkness in his eyes that masked whatever emotions were washing through him.

She wasn't afraid, because she knew he would never physically hurt her. And because she'd never loved anyone the way she'd loved Jake. Never wanted anyone the way she'd always wanted him.

Christy stood perfectly still, consciously not letting him see any of this. She might still love him, want him, but thankfully she possessed a certain measure of self-protective instincts.

She could feel her pulse beating rapidly in her throat. Where merely seconds before she'd been cold, now she was hot, flushed, burning, and all from the touch of his hand on her arm.

He was looking at her, taking in the sight of her naked body, and she fought the urge to cover herself. After all, he was the intruder here. He was on her turf, and he owed her an explanation.

She moved away from him.

He tightened his grip on her arm.

"Let me go," she said, her voice low. She couldn't take much more of him touching her without revealing just what that touch was doing to her emotions.

He stepped closer, not releasing her. She looked up at him, and saw that he'd changed. Profoundly. All traces of the boy she'd loved, the boy she'd come of age with, were gone. In their place were the hard contours of a man's face, the muscled strength of a male in the prime of his life. She could feel the energy radiating from him, the anger. Every inch of her skin, every nerve in her body, was aware of his intense presence.

She felt his fingers as he held her head, felt them twine through her wet hair, knew that he was going to angle her head, kiss her—

She closed her eyes at the savage, angry look on his face, just before his lips met hers.

It all came flooding back, and in that instant she knew she had to have Jake back in her life, had to be close to him, lie next to him, feel him inside her, his hands touching her, one last time.

But she couldn't let it happen. She'd let him go once, and it had almost destroyed her. It had destroyed parts of her life. Most of it. Now, if she gave in again, as much as her body, as her emotions might want to, she instinctively knew she would do herself irreparable damage. She'd never recover.

He must have sensed the change in her when he drew back. She looked up at him, knowing her heart had to be in her eyes, knowing how well he knew her, could read her. If he saw any of what she felt, he'd turn around and leave. Now. And she would run toward safety and contentment with Arthur Beck.

She forced herself to pull away from him one last time.

He held firm.

"I can't let you go," he whispered.

THE HOUSE was dark, the only lights she'd turned on were in the kitchen, on the ground floor. Jake mounted the stairs, and Christy kept her eyes closed to ward off any dizziness. He'd slung her over his shoulder and now was ascending toward the bedroom. She knew what he wanted, what was going to happen. She knew he was angry, and knew she'd given him a reason for that anger the way she'd ended their relationship.

But to have stayed angry for twelve years?

Yet she hadn't been able to move on, either.

He started down the wide hall, and headed straight for the master bedroom. Done all in white, it was as starkly modern as the rest of Rutger's house. The huge, king-size bed was on the far wall, the bed frame black metal and streamlined.

He dumped her on the bed.

She started to scramble away.

He pinned her down.

She struggled. Not as much out of fear as with a desperate sense of having to get away from him, from his touch, his scent, the overwhelming effect he had on her senses.

Out of the corner of her eye, she caught movement. Jake had glanced into the open drawer of the bedside table, and now took something out of it.

She struggled harder.

He easily mastered her, moving her toward the bottom of the bed. Sliding her along the cool, woven cotton bedspread. Then she felt something cold and metallic around her ankle, heard a snap—

"Damn it, Jake!"

He'd handcuffed her to the foot of the bed. To the metal bed frame. And as she watched him, he slipped the key into the pocket of his black jeans.

"This has gone far enough!" She tried to inject her words with a confidence she was far from feeling.

"Oh, I don't think so."

Her breathing hurt, felt rapid and uneven. She couldn't look at him. She closed her eyes.

"Christy."

That voice. Rough and deep with emotion. For one horrible moment she thought she was going to cry.

"Christy, look at me."

She couldn't.

"I have to finish it, Christy." She could feel his pause, hear him slowly walk away from the bed, then the sounds of his boots hitting the floor.

"I have to finish it. Get you out of my system. Get to the truth. And get on with my life."

And destroy me in the process.

She opened her eyes. Chanced a glance. He was slipping his black T-shirt over his head, and she saw the strong chest, corded with muscles. Jake had never consciously worked out, but he'd always been physically active. He hadn't gone soft, as so many men did, but possessed a body that made her mouth go dry.

"Don't," she said softly, putting out a hand in front of her. Hoping she might be able to make him listen, and at the same time knowing there was nothing that was going to divert him from taking what he wanted.

But there was absolutely no remorse in his expression. Nothing that would lead her to believe he would soften in his resolve. This was something that had to be played out.

"I don't want you. Not this way."

He was unfastening his jeans, then skimming them and his briefs over his hips. She averted her eyes, but not before she saw his strong arousal.

"We'll make a deal," he said, his voice low. Soft. Deadly. For one wild moment, she thought he was like an animal stalking its prey, intent on it for that moment before moving in for the kill.

"No deals," she said, but her voice sounded weak to her own ears.

"We'll make a deal," he said, and it was as if he hadn't heard her. "I won't do anything to you that you don't want me to do."

Oh, he knew her so well. Knew that a part of her would go up in flames the second he touched her. Knew that he'd haunted her dreams during countless, restless, aching nights.

"Jake," she began.

"No."

Then he was on the bed, over her, and as Christy looked up into the hard, uncompromising expression on his face, she knew that more had changed within Jake than simply the journey from boy to man. She realized that what she'd done to him, so long ago, had eaten away at him, had created this hunger, this anger, this desire for first revenge and then closure.

She glanced away, desperate to break their contact.

He took a handful of her damp hair as leverage, then twisted it in his fingers, forced her head around toward his, forced her to meet his gaze.

Tears filled her eyes, not at the slight pain, but at the emotional intensity of their situation.

"Jake, please . . ."

"I needed you," he whispered. His eyes, so very blue, were so close, so intense. He studied her face as if trying to memorize it, catalog changes, really see her, see inside her.

"I needed you then," he whispered. "And God help me, I need you now."

He pulled her toward him, flattening her against the hard muscled wall of his chest. She put up her hands to ward him off, pushed at his arms, tried to get out of his hold, tried to create distance between them.

And then it happened.

Her body simply betrayed her. As if in one of the erotic dreams that had tortured her nights, her hands slid up his chest, entwined around his neck, then into his hair.

"Damn you," he whispered, then buried his face in her hair.

They lay like that for long seconds. She could feel the frantic beating of his heart, the burning heat and strong length of his erection.

She spoke his name softly, one last plea, one last attempt to make him realize what he was about to do to her.

"No," he said against her ear, and she felt the mattress sag as he moved his body over hers. "You can't ask me to wait, Christy." He kissed the side of her neck and her head fell back. She bit her lip, not wanting him to hear the soft moan that threatened to escape.

She didn't want him to wait. She was terrified, out of control, totally run by her emotions, by her body, and a part of her wanted this to happen. Had dreamed of it.

She did moan then, as he slid lower, as his lips found first one nipple, then the other. They tightened painfully, into hard little buds, and he lightly brushed his fingertips over them, bringing them to aching, straining attention.

She reached for him, but he caught her wrists with his fingers. And she understood, dimly, with the small part of her rational mind that was still functioning, that he was going to make love to her, to reduce her to a woman who would end up begging for her final release. He was going to stay in control, and try to burn her out of his memory.

"Jake," she whispered, and this time meant to ask him to let her touch him, know him, pleasure him.

"No," he said, then kissed her roughly. "No, I've waited long enough."

He'd misunderstood her. But he wasn't completely in control. She could sense it. Jake had normally been one of the most passionate of lovers, taking his time, making sure she was with him each and every step of the way. Now his impatience betrayed his lack of control where she was concerned.

His hands molded her hips, pressing her against his body, against his arousal. Then she felt one hand against her inner thigh, pushing it up, apart from the other, finding her. Her face flushed crimson as she realized how ready she was for Jake. And what that revealed to him.

"Tell me, Christy," he whispered as he began to kiss his way down her stomach. "Tell me."

She couldn't get a sound out of her mouth, her throat was so tight with emotion, with arousal. Her head fell back. She tried to move away from his relentless assault, but he had her wrists in one hand and the other was stroking her, first high on the inner thigh, then around but never directly on the area she wanted him to touch.

Then he did. Her hips bucked, and she heard the masculine triumph in his voice.

"Tell me, Christy. Tell me to stop."

She couldn't. She wanted him so badly. There had never been a man who had made her feel as much as Jake did. Ever. The two brief affairs she'd had over the twelve years they'd been apart had left her cold.

He slowly eased one finger inside her, then two.

She responded, clenching delicate inner muscles around him, the response involuntary and almost physically painful. She was ready for him, for whatever he wanted to do to her. And she knew, in her heart, that she could deny him nothing.

He stroked her as he slid his fingers inside her, stroked that part of her that burned, that wanted, that demanded his touch. Her hips moved, arching toward his fingers, and he slid his hand away and kissed her, deeply, the most intimate kiss of all.

A sob broke out of her, then another as she struggled against giving over to him. Then he would have her, then he could do whatever he wanted. Then he could break her heart, and that scared her more than anything. Because too much had already happened between them. There were too many secrets for them to ever be free of the past.

He knew her. Knew what she liked. He let go of her hands and she grabbed his head, twined her fingers in his hair, pulled him against her. He used both his free hands to spread her legs even wider, and she felt sensation building, burning, then that delicious inevitability...

She fell over the edge, her hips bucking, tears running down her cheeks, a low moan of total feminine surrender leaving her before she could bite her lip and try to contain it. But he knew.

She didn't know how long she lay there afterward, how long she'd closed her eyes and simply floated in the aftermath. When she opened her eyes, he was lying next to her. Watching her.

She looked away as hot color stained her cheeks. Here she was, lying in bed with the one man on earth who knew her more intimately than anyone else, and she was embarrassed.

But he wasn't the Jake she'd known. This man was more like a stranger. She remembered Jake's smile, and all she felt from this man was controlled coldness. Anger.

He put an arm around her, pulled her against him. They were tucked together like spoons, so she couldn't see his face. She closed her eyes as more tears threatened to escape. For just an instant, he'd felt like the old Jake, the way they used to lie together in bed for hours, the way he used to hold her.

This was emotional torture.

She snuggled against him, then felt the hard, hot pressure of his erection. She froze, then adjusted herself so their lower bodies didn't come into contact. And wondered what he was going to do.

"Tell me what you want," he whispered into her hair.

Her body felt so soft, so warm, so sensually pliable. She'd always loved that delicious melting feeling afterward, when she'd been satiated and safe in Jake's arms. When she'd known he loved her.

This man would never love her again.

She turned to face him, adjusting her ankle carefully against the constraints of the handcuffs.

"Jake," she said, and reached up to touch his face.

Something flickered in his eyes. Changed. Then he took her hand in his, away from his cheek. His eyes were so blue, so intent, he didn't look away from her and she felt helpless to break the contact.

"Touch me," he whispered.

She did, taking the hard, hot length into her hands, stroking it, remembering. She'd loved his body, and all he'd taught her about her own. She'd come to Jake a virgin, so long ago, and he'd nurtured her sensuality, opened her up to sensation, made her his in a way no other man ever would or could.

She touched him gently, softly. Remembering how it had always been between them, that sexual wildfire that sprang up so effortlessly. Her fingers gently increased their pressure, then she was stroking him, watching the changes in his face, taking a certain perverse, feminine pleasure in how she could control him this way, if for only a short time.

The lines around his mouth deepened, his entire body tensed as she pleasured him. His eyes closed, and she impulsively moved lower, then kissed his hairroughened stomach. The muscles jumped, and she rested her cheek against his belly.

"Christy." There was a warning in his voice.

She chose to ignore it.

"Do you want me to?" she whispered, not daring to look up at him.

His answer was to thread his fingers through her hair and gently guide her toward the proudly erect shaft.

She didn't take him in her mouth right away. Being close to him this way made her feel incredibly vulnerable, for him as well. She pressed her cheek against the hard, hot, aroused flesh and heard his quick intake of breath.

His fingers tightened in her hair, but didn't force her to do anything. She rubbed her face against him, took him in her hands, then slowly began to kiss the aroused flesh.

This was true power. He might leave her after this night, after he'd got what he'd apparently come for, but she would make him leave with memories she hoped would give him as many agonized dreams as she'd suffered through in the years they'd been apart.

She knew what he liked in the way a woman could only with a man she'd been with for a long time. Her mouth closed over him, she heard a deep, rumbling groan issue from his chest, and almost smiled. This was Jake, not some arrogant stranger. This was the Jake she remembered.

She kept the rhythm strong and steady, teasing him, tormenting him, keeping him off guard. And she felt the signs of his increasing arousal, knew he wouldn't be able to hold out much longer, not with pleasure this intense.

At the exact moment she thought he wouldn't be able to stand much more, she raised herself up over his body, intending to straddle him and bring him to completion—and the restraints of the handcuff brought her up short.

She glanced up at him, totally frustrated, and for a heartstopping instant saw the old Jake, the laughter in his blue eyes, the fondness as he looked at her.

"Take this off me."

He rolled over so he was on top of her, pinning her against the soft mattress, his weight on his forearms.

He kissed her on the neck, just below her ear. She shivered.

"Promise not to run?"

She nodded.

"I'll track you down if you do."

"I know." She reached up and smoothed the hair back from his forehead. Once again he caught her hand, as if the gesture was too unbearably intimate, as if he didn't want to go all the way back in time to when they'd been so close.

That hurt. But she simply left her hand in his and looked away.

"Promise?"

She nodded.

He got up, took the key out of his jeans pocket, then unlocked the handcuff. It fell away from her ankle and he took it in his hands, rubbing his fingers over the skin that had touched the cold metal.

"I didn't know you were into bondage," she said.

"I'm not. Only when the woman in question is incredibly stubborn. And can't be trusted."

So that's what he thinks of you.

Then she didn't think at all as he pulled her against him, covered her mouth with his, gave her a series of long, drugging kisses. This wasn't punishment, this was erotic ecstasy. Her mind seemed to go completely blank, leaving her with only the demands of her senses, of the flesh.

His hands were everywhere, on her breasts, her hips, her back, her buttocks. His kisses followed the path his hands had taken, leaving her highly sensitized, wanting, waiting . . .

Jake rolled over on his back, taking her with him so she was astride him as before.

"Is this what you want?" he whispered, cupping the side of her face in his large hand.

She shook her head, then linked her arms around his neck. She slid to the side, rolling, taking him with her, repositioning them so he was on top of her, above her. She wanted him in charge, wanted him in control, wanted him to be the dominant one this time.

"Please, Jake," she whispered. "Please."

He didn't disappoint her. He never had. With one sure thrust he was inside her, then swiftly building her pleasure to levels almost unendurable. She moaned, but he cut the sound off with a hard kiss, pressing deeper, thrusting strongly, taking possession in the savage way of a man who had been denied too long.

He covered her completely and she reveled in the press of his naked flesh against hers, the weight of his overheated, strongly muscled body. She felt that wonderful ascent start, that pressure, that burning ache, and closed her eyes, her head turning first to one side, then the other.

"Look at me." Jake took his weight on his forearms so he could see her face.

She couldn't open her eyes for an instant, the feelings were so intense.

"Look at me," he whispered, threading his fingers through her hair, holding her head so she had to gaze up at him. "I want to see you, Christy."

She opened her eyes and felt the love she had for this man flow out of her, toward him, enveloping both of them. And she knew at that exact instant that she would never belong to another man, would never know another man this way, would never marry Arthur.

His blue eyes watched her, his hard mouth curving up into a half smile when one of his deep strokes caused her to catch her breath.

"You like that?"

She nodded.

He pushed in again, just as deeply, and she caught her breath again, started to close her eyes.

"No," he said, his voice low. Strained. He was fighting for control now, wanting to give her as much pleasure as possible before he found his own release. "Don't close your eyes."

She kept them open, looking directly at him at this most intimate moment.

He kissed the corner of her mouth as he continued to pump strongly in and out of her. The smile caught his mouth again, and she saw the old Jake, the man she'd loved with all her heart.

His voice was low and rough when he spoke again. "I want to see you when you come."

His words sent her over the edge, and he followed her. The climax was so powerful she thought she might pass out, but she vaguely felt Jake easing her against him, draping one strong leg over both of hers, an arm around her waist. He didn't even bother with covers, they both simply lay on the bedspread.

Just before exhaustion, both physical and emotional, claimed her, Christy felt a great tremor shake his body. He'd been as affected by this as she had. Her breathing deepened, she felt their heartbeats fall into a similar rhythm. And she fell asleep with her head on his chest, a soft smile on her face.

4

Thirteen years ago . . .

HER INTUITION had been right. She could tell Jake anything. They grew closer as the months went by, and Christy's insecurities, her feelings that he would date her for a few weeks and then dump her, faded into nothingness.

For Jake seemed happy.

They fell into a routine. Meeting for lunch every day. He picked her up in the mornings in his Mustang and drove her home from school. Sometimes they met at the library and did homework, sometimes they took off right after class and headed for one of the Indian Canyons on the outskirts of town.

It didn't really matter, as long as they were together.

They got to know each other. She learned that his parents had died in a plane crash when he was twelve, and Jake had been raised by his older sister, Hannah, until he was sixteen. At that time, she'd wanted to marry and her fiancé had been offered a job overseas. Jake had elected to stay in the States. It wasn't that he didn't love his sister, and it wasn't that she hadn't done an excellent job taking care of him. It was simply that he saw the need for her to finally make a life for herself.

He was the most mature seventeen-year-old she'd ever met. While the other boys at school that age seemed hopelessly immature, Jake knew what he wanted and went after it. He held a part-time job after school at a local garage, and was an absolute genius working with cars. He could listen to an automobile drive by and tell you what was wrong with it simply from the sound. His boss liked him because he was reliable, and he held his own with men twice his age.

That weekly salary, along with some money his sister sent him each month, enabled him to support himself. He lived in a small apartment right around the corner from the garage, and that was where they spent a certain amount of time—but not too much, and never late at night.

She knew why. Jake was protecting her. He knew what would inevitably happen if they spent a lot of time together, alone. Relying on her instincts once again, Christy knew he'd seen more of life than she had, that he was experienced—a lot more. And he'd never believed the popular assessment of her, that she'd lived fast and was easy. He protected her, and she loved him for it.

She eventually even told him about her father. And her mother. Her mother had died when she was seven, and other than a faded photo, Christy didn't have much to remember. There were no aunts, uncles or cousins to help keep memories alive, and her father had found his solace in the bottom of a bottle.

Jake knew about that, and sympathized. The few times he'd met her father, he'd been quiet and respectful, but those sharp blue eyes had taken in everything. Including the way Christy managed the household, from cleaning to cooking to the finances. The small apartment they lived in was always immaculate, meals hot and on time, money squirreled away so her father couldn't spend it all on liquor. He spent most of his life in his reclining chair, his attention on the television. Her tabby cat, Boots, completed their small household.

She had the feeling that Jake observed a lot more than he let on. He wasn't one to talk much, but she knew his mind was always working. He observed, and almost always went with what his hard-won experience had taught him, as opposed to popular opinion.

Six months into their relationship, he gave her his class ring. She'd been thrilled, wrapped it with yarn so it fit her finger, and had been so proud to wear it to school. Now she was convinced her life was changing. Now things would be different. Jake had come into her life for a reason, it was almost as if he'd been sent to her. She wasn't going to let him down.

She took a part-time job as well, at a local drugstore. Instead of spending her salary on clothes and makeup, she deposited it in her savings account. She wanted to be responsible, wanted Jake to know that, whatever his dreams were, she would help him achieve them every step of the way.

She turned seventeen in October. Her father didn't remember, and she didn't remind him. She and Jake went out to dinner, and back to his apartment at the end of the evening, where he gave her his present.

"Open it," he said, smiling at her nervousness.

She couldn't seem to make her fingers move, to tear the paper, pull at the ribbons and tape. The box was medium-size, but curiously light. Finally, getting her fumbling nervousness under control, she began to tear at the wrapping paper.

Jake was so self-sufficient in a funny sort of way. They'd gone to a local steak house for dinner, but saved dessert for his apartment. He'd bought a cake for her at one of the local gourmet groceries, chocolate and more chocolate, her favorite. It sat on the small table in the kitchen, seventeen candles stuck in the glossy frosting.

Christy opened the cardboard box and found a mass of shredded packing material.

"Very funny."

"There's something in there." Now he seemed nervous, but she couldn't have guessed why.

She fished around within the shreds of packing material until her fingers closed around a small box. Her heart went perfectly still. A jewelry box. Small. It could only be a ring.

Jake watched her closely, and she could feel his eyes on her as she took the small jeweler's box out of the package and opened it.

A ring. Gold. With a tiny diamond.

She knew what it meant, and she didn't know what to say. Couldn't say anything. Her throat closed, making speech impossible. She looked up at him, knew tears were filling her eyes, and threw her arms around his neck.

"I take it that's a yes?" he said, his voice muffled against her hair.

She nodded her head.

After a moment, he took her hand and slipped the ring onto her finger.

"I'll have enough money in a while to get you a better one—"

She shook her head. "This is fine."

"No, Christy, you deserve something a little better than—" he grinned self-deprecatingly "—the smallest diamond the jeweler had to offer. He said it was more like a friendship ring than an actual engagement ring."

"Like an . . . engaged to be engaged ring."

He nodded, then shifted so he was kneeling on the floor in front of her, facing her on the couch.

"I'm going to do this properly," he said, grinning up at her, taking her hand.

Her eyes flooded with tears again, this time they spilled down her cheeks. She wiped them away with her free hand, smiling the whole time.

"Christy, will you marry me?"

"Yes!" She threw herself into his arms, and they fell over onto the shag carpeting. "Yes, yes, yes!"

She never remembered cutting or eating her cake, or what they did the rest of the night. They talked and talked about the future, about Jake's dreams of going to Los Angeles and trying to make it as an actor. Her dreams were his, wherever he was. He took her home that night, dropped her off on her doorstep with another kiss and she walked into the cigarette-smoke-filled living room feeling as if she were so suffused with happiness that nothing better could happen to her.

"HEY, JAKE, that's a good-looking little *chiquita* you've got."

Christy stopped, then stilled, almost to the doorway of the main garage. She met Jake here a few times a week, but now hesitated, wondering if she'd embarrass him by walking in at that exact moment.

"Shut up, Ross." Jake sounded tense.

She could picture Ross; she saw him almost every time she stopped in to see Jake. The man was naturally aggressive, a little banty rooster with sandy blond hair and hazel eyes. Unhappily married with three children, he'd always made her feel slightly uneasy with all his macho posturing.

"What? Hey man, I'm *complimenting* you on your good taste. If I had a woman with an ass like that, not to mention those—"

She heard the sounds of a scuffle, then Ross's voice as the swift fight broke.

"Jesus, Jake, okay, I'm sorry—"

"Don't talk about her like that. Just *don't*."

When Ross spoke again, Christy could hear the slyness in his inflection.

"I get it. But I guess you're not."

"Shut up."

"She's not giving you any of what she's got. That's why you're always in such a bad mood—"

"Shut up!"

"I feel sorry for you, man. You've got yourself a little tease—"

Another scuffle ensued, until Bob, the owner, put a stop to it. Christy walked quietly out the side of the work area, to the back of the station by the rest rooms. The hot afternoon desert sun beat down on her, she could feel the sweat starting to form around her hairline, but she didn't feel any discomfort.

She wasn't a tease. She knew that. Whenever she and Jake had been intimate together, he'd always stopped things before they got completely out of control. He'd never even touched her below the waist, even though both of them had become so physically aroused there had been times it had been hard to stop.

She'd wondered why he wanted to stop, because he had to know she'd never deny him anything. He was a year older than she was, but much older in other ways. Street smart. More experienced. She didn't know how she knew, but she knew Jake wasn't a virgin. And he knew she was, because she'd told him.

He was eighteen, at an age when most boys were obsessed with making a conquest. Getting as much as they could. And worse, he'd already experienced what a woman had to offer a man physically, so knowing had to make waiting that much more difficult for him. He knew what he was missing.

She would have given him anything he wanted even before he'd proposed. Even before their friendship ring. So now she didn't understand what he was waiting for. She was seventeen, but she'd been with him almost a year. In her own way, she'd grown up pretty fast. The world didn't hold a whole lot of illusions for her. She knew that happiness was elusive, and at that moment, Christy knew there was nothing she wanted more than to make love with Jake, to show him how much she loved him.

If he was waiting for her to make a decision, then she'd just made it.

She went into the ladies room, released her hair from its band and brushed it, then refastened it. She freshened her makeup. Ross's comments had disturbed her, but Christy wasn't so naive that she didn't know what he was talking about. She knew she had a body made for sin. Before Jake, her early development had made her self-conscious, along with all the unwanted attention she'd received from men.

Now, because of Jake and their love for each other, she felt proud of her body. She wanted to offer herself to him. She wanted him to be happy, and she knew he would make sure the whole intimate experience would be good for her as well.

She studied her outfit, wanting to make sure there was no truth to what Ross had said. Jeans. Tight jeans, but not because of any deliberate effort to provoke. They were simply old, well-worn and fit like a second skin. The pale yellow knit top was also faded—she didn't have a whole lot of money for clothes. It was a little too tight from repeated washings, but not blatantly so.

Her long blond hair was pulled back in a ponytail, and the only makeup she wore was a little brown mascara and some pink gloss. She'd toned down the black raccoon eyes look soon after meeting Jake. More than anything, she hadn't wanted him to think of her as cheap.

To hell with Ross and whatever was going on in his mind, she thought as she picked up her small backpack and a few textbooks, then walked outside into the bright sunshine.

When she entered the cool shade of the garage, it was as if the scene she'd overheard earlier had never happened. Jake was on the phone, talking to a customer, Ross underneath a Ford Taurus, tinkering. Bob was in the back office, watching everything through the large glass window, his Coke-bottle-lens glasses low on his nose. The gray-haired man waved when he saw her, his smile genuine.

Christy waved back. She liked Bob and didn't want to cause Jake any trouble on the job.

Jake gave her a nod of acknowledgment, his attention still on the customer on the phone. But as soon as he finished the call and put the customer's chart on the main desk, he came toward her. Because she was looking for it, she could see the tension in his expression, the tight lines around his mouth, the anger in his dark blue eyes.

"Hey." He didn't touch her, and she knew it was because he was covered with grime. But Jake would have looked good in anything, dirty or not, and she thought he looked wonderful in his dark gray coveralls.

"Hey." She reached up, touched his cheek, gave him a quick kiss. "How's it going?"

"Same old stuff." He frowned. "You working tonight?"

"Yeah. Until ten. But then I have the next two days off."

"I've got tomorrow off. We should do something."

A plan began to form in her mind. Jake would never know what hit him.

"Okay." She glanced down, conscious of someone watching. Ross had scooted out from beneath the car he was working on, and was gazing at her with interest in his hazel eyes. She knew that look, and disliked it.

"Hey." Jake had obviously followed her gaze and saw what was happening. "Work on the car, okay?"

"I don't envy you, bud." Ross ran a hand through his sandy blond hair, then began to whistle as he slid back beneath the Taurus.

"What does that mean?" she asked, even though she knew.

"Another one of Ross's delusions," Jake said easily. "So you'll get dinner at work?"

"I'll just grab a slice of pizza on my break."

"Yeah. I'll probably pick up a sandwich."

"Okay. I'm going to get going."

"Take the car."

She liked the way he referred to his car, the black Mustang, as *the* car, not *my* car. It was his, bought and paid for, but the way he talked about it made it seem they were already a team, working together.

"No, it's not that far to walk."

"Take it. I'll still be cleaning up by the time you get off. You can pick me up."

He reached into his pocket and tossed her the keys. She smiled up at him, kissed him again, then walked out the door, closing her ears to Ross's whispered, *"Va-va-voom!"*

AT WORK that night, on her break, she tried to hide the condoms and foam among a few other purchases. A magazine, some more lip gloss, shampoo and two candy bars. Mascara, a facial mask and a paperback novel.

Picking them out had been difficult enough. Ribbed, nonribbed, different colors, different *fla-*

vors—she hadn't known what she was doing, so she picked up three boxes, all different, praying the entire time that a smart-assed clerk wouldn't look at her and say something like, "Planning quite a night, aren't you?"

Because she was.

Once she'd made her purchases, she went out to the car and put the condoms and foam into her backpack, leaving the rest of the stuff in the bag. She even went so far as to take the receipt and dispose of it, so Jake wouldn't see it. Not that he would have gone looking inside the bag to begin with, but her senses were heightened and she was totally paranoid.

She never ate that slice of pizza. Too nervous.

At the end of the evening, she had to count her cash drawer out three times before it balanced. She, who usually came out to the penny. If her boss noticed, she didn't make any comment.

Then she was back out in the Mustang, heading for the garage.

Jake was tired when she picked him up.

"Bad day?" she said as she eased the car out on the main road.

"Not one of my best." His eyes were closed, and he was leaning back on the headrest. She felt for him. He started work at two and worked long hours. He was saving money for the dream, the money they would need when they both moved to Los Angeles. He was determined, and a hard worker. Nothing usually got Jake down, so it worried her he was this exhausted.

"Did you eat?"

He shook his head.

She pulled into a taco stand, and they took food back to his place.

"Don't you want me to drop you off?" he questioned as they didn't take the turn that would lead to her apartment.

"Nope. I left one of my books at your place." The lie slid off her tongue, and she wondered at how easy it was.

"Okay."

They got back to his apartment and ate their late dinner. Then Christy turned on the news while she cleaned up the kitchen. Jake was already sprawled out on the couch, and when she walked into the living room, he was fast asleep.

She switched off the television, locked the door, closed the curtains and turned off the bell on the phone. Then she stripped down to her underwear, took the condoms and foam out of her backpack and placed them on the old, scarred coffee table. She found a warm blanket and covered Jake with it. He seemed so totally exhausted that he didn't even wake when she maneuvered his head onto a pillow.

Then, taking a deep breath, she climbed beneath the blanket and lay down next to him.

SHE COULDN'T sleep, she was so apprehensive. Scared. But excited at the same time. She'd thought of the moment she would finally lose her virginity, and she'd never doubted it would be with Jake. But now that the moment was here, she was a little—a lot—nervous.

He shifted in his sleep, said something, then stilled. She smiled into the darkness. She'd never spent a night with him—they really hadn't spent a lot of time alone in his apartment. That was when she'd known he had more experience than she did. He was aware of the consequences of their actions, and always thought to protect her.

Now she would do the same for him. Protect him from his own sense of sacrifice. If they were going to get married eventually, what was to stop them from loving each other in the most intimate way of all?

Impatient for him to wake up and discover her, Christy found herself slowly unbuttoning his shirt, then sliding it apart. She loved Jake's bare chest, all muscles and crisp, curly hair. She loved the warmth of his scent. Ever so gently, she leaned forward in the dark and pressed her lips to his bare chest.

He didn't respond.

She moved her hands lower, to the fastening of his jeans. She'd removed his shoes and socks when he'd fallen asleep on the couch, but hadn't touched the rest of his clothing. Now she slowly unfastened his jeans, then slid her fingers beneath the soft, worn denim. Then farther still, beneath his briefs, until she came in contact with hot, hair-roughened skin.

The minute she touched his sex it began to respond, to grow larger against her hand, to swell and become stiffly erect. She'd touched him through his clothing before, but he'd always stopped her at that point. As if he knew where his control could be broken and never wanted to reach that point.

He groaned softly in his sleep, then turned toward her and took her in his arms, pulling her tightly against him. But he was still half-asleep, and Christy knew he didn't have a clue as to what was really going on.

She managed to reach in front and unfasten her bra, then wriggle out of it. Now she was lying on the couch with him with only a pair of lacy panties between her and total nakedness.

He couldn't possibly stop now.

She didn't want him to.

He came awake slowly, his hands touching her, his body pressing against hers. She saw, in the dim light from the kitchen, slow realization come into his eyes, suffuse his expression.

"Christy?"

She put a finger over his lips.

"Please," she whispered. She reached down and touched him, saw the faint tremors that shook his body before he took her hand in his and moved it to his chest.

He didn't speak, only looked at her.

At that moment, she knew it wasn't going to happen.

"Please," she whispered again, her eyes starting to fill. "I want—"

"Christy." He reached down and fastened his jeans, then pulled her into his arms and held her tightly. "Christy, you don't have to do this."

"I want to," she said fiercely.

"Then why are you shaking?"

He knew her too well. Everything had gone wrong. Frustrated and overwhelmed, she started to cry.

"Don't," he said, soothing her with both the tone of his voice and the touch of his hands. "Don't cry, baby. Don't cry."

"You don't want me . . ."

She felt the sigh that reverberated throughout his body. "Oh, you have no idea."

"Then why—"

"Christy." He sat up on the sofa, maneuvering his body so there was a little more space between them even though he still held her. He slid his shirt off, then helped her put it on, fastening just two of the buttons. Then he held her again, his chin on top of her head as he spoke.

"I don't want it to be like this. Something you feel you have to do, something fast and . . . furtive. I wanted to wait until we got married. I never wanted you to feel—"

He was searching for the right words, and all of a sudden it dawned on her what he'd been trying to do. When he'd met her, she'd been the bad girl, the fast girl, the girl with the reputation. He was trying to put that to rest, to reassure her that he considered her virginity something special. That she was special.

She felt as if she might burst with love for him.

"But it's not good for you," she whispered against his chest. "Being tense. Everyone can see it but me, and—"

"Whoa. Whoa. Wait. What are you talking about?"

She'd overstepped. Revealed too much. She felt his hand come up beneath her chin, tilt her head so he could look into her eyes.

"When did you get to the station today?"

The lies didn't come so easily when he was looking her in the eye. She couldn't deceive him.

"I heard . . . what Ross said . . ."

"He's a jerk."

"But it's true, it's not good for you—"

He kissed her. "Not true."

"But—"

He kissed her again. "Give me some credit for knowing what I want."

"Do you want to make love to me?"

"Oh, yeah." His blue eyes were shining, that look in them that she loved.

"Then why can't we just do it?"

He passed a hand over his eyes. "I've got to be crazy," he muttered.

"I think so."

He glanced at her then, and she deliberately unfastened the two buttons of his shirt, letting the material fall to the sides. She heard the short intake of his breath.

"Christy, don't."

"There's condoms and foam on the coffee table. I picked them up at work tonight. Several brands, because I didn't know which ones you liked." She didn't know where she got the courage to do what she did next, but she lifted her hips and slowly rolled her panties down.

He couldn't stop watching her. He closed his eyes for a minute, then looked away.

"You're sure?" he said quietly.

"More sure than I've been of anything else in my life."

"You won't regret it later?"

"The only regret I'll have is if you don't make love to me."

"Damn it, Christy!" He moved so quickly she was shocked, but he suddenly had her pinned down on the soft couch, his body on top of hers, holding her face in both his hands, staring into her eyes.

"Is this about you, or about me?"

She wet her lips nervously. "I don't want you to be frustrated anymore, Jake."

"Then it's about me. And that's not good enough."

"No." She grabbed him, grasped his shoulders, held him to her before he could get up. "No, it's about me, too. I want to know, Jake. I want to discover it all with you. I—I don't want to *not* know anymore. Sometimes, when we stop, it leaves me so frustrated, but even more than physically frustrated because I don't know what it is that I want."

His eyes narrowed as he studied her. "You have to know what happens."

"Yeah, I do. But not with you. Not the way it would feel, the way it would be. That's what I want to know, and I'm scared but I want it to happen at the same time, I almost want you to *make* it happen. To be the one in charge, to let me know. Because I only want to know about it with you. No one else, *ever*."

Something in his eyes shifted. Something indefinable. But she knew she'd reached him.

"All right."

Now she was nervous.

"Christy?"

She had to meet his eyes.

"You can stop me at any time."

She nodded.

"It won't give me any pleasure at all to know you did something you didn't want to do."

She nodded again.

"You've got to trust me."

"I do."

He kissed her. Kissed her again. Only this time it was so different because she knew he wasn't going to stop. Not until they were finished.

He stripped the shirt off her, and she lay naked on the couch. The lights were off, the only illumination coming from the soft light in the small kitchen. Jake kept his jeans on, but lay down on top of her, positioning himself so he lay in the cradle of her thighs. She could feel his hard erection pressing into her belly.

It wasn't quite the same as before, because this time she was so much more aware of his size and strength. His kisses were longer, the caresses of his hands as he smoothed them over her body were stronger. She knew he was preparing her, readying her for what lay ahead.

He moved to her breasts, kissing, licking, softly biting. Arousing her. Teasing her. Until she grasped his head in her hands, pulling his hair, desperate for something she'd never known until tonight.

Then he moved lower, kissing, caressing. She could feel the muscles in her stomach quiver and jump as he kissed them, as he moved relentlessly lower, pushing her thighs apart—

Her hips bucked in response as he kissed her there, that most intimate place. She closed her eyes, clenched her fists as sensations she'd never felt before flooded her body. She'd thought she would melt, relax, burn hotter and hotter, but this was as if she was some sort of spring, coiling tighter and tighter, ever tighter—

He brushed his fingers over her feminine mound and she cried out, then bit her lip, embarrassed by the noise. She felt him slowly part her, then ease a finger up inside her, so gently, so slowly...

He slid up beside her then, still moving his hand, rubbing her, touching her, sliding that finger in and out. He kissed her, stroked her hair back from her flushed face. Just as she became used to the feeling of fullness, she felt another finger search, part her, enter her. Now both fingers moved inside her, stretching her gently, readying her for what was to come.

She thought it would happen then, but Jake seemed to be in no hurry. He stroked her for what seemed to be an endless time, all the while kissing her lips, her neck, her breasts, then back up to her mouth, sucking her lower lip into his mouth, thrusting his tongue inside with that same slow, sensuous rhythm that matched what he was doing with his hand.

She whimpered against his kiss and he shifted his body, curving a leg over her so she couldn't move away as the movement of his hand became subtly faster, as the sensations between her thighs began to burn much hotter and wetter. She tensed against the escalation of feeling, then felt his lips against her ear.

"Just let go, baby. Just let go."

She could barely hear him, she was so lost in sensation.

"Let go. I'll catch you. I'll catch you, baby."

It happened then, that most exquisite of feminine explosions, then contractions around his fingers, which still moved against her even as she came. She started to cry, and he turned her face against his chest, held her throughout the rest of it, pulled her tightly against him.

Her body felt boneless. So tired. Vulnerable. All the tension of the evening caught up with her, all the exhaustion that had come with holding in her fears. But she felt so very good, and so close to him, with what they'd just shared. Christy smiled up at him and caught his brilliant, possessive gaze.

"Jake?"

"Mmm." He was smiling as he nuzzled her hair, then kissed her. She wore his class ring on a chain between her breasts, and now he moved it aside and kissed her there as well. And she realized he would slow it all down for her, give her all the time she needed to assimilate this.

"Thank you," she whispered, her head pillowed against the strong muscles of his chest. Then she fell asleep.

5

Friday morning, Memorial Day Weekend

JAKE WOKE with the immediate knowledge that he was still in bed with Christy. He didn't move, simply lay in Rutger's huge bed and enjoyed the feel of her body next to his. She slept as if she were exhausted, and he knew the feeling. If she'd decided to escape in the middle of the night, he wasn't sure if he would have gone after her. Not right that minute. Oh, he would have found her eventually, but he was as overcome as she was by what had happened last night.

Why had he let things get so out of control? When he'd envisioned coming face-to-face with Christy again, it had been with the intent of showing her how well he'd done without her, how he hadn't needed her—when the truth was that not a day went by when he hadn't missed her. Wanted her.

Loved her.

She was the one person on the face of this earth who could cause him to completely lose control, and it wasn't something he was proud of. Like last night. Granted, he hadn't known she was going to strip down and dive into the pool, and he'd never been that rational around her naked body. But he should have been able to keep things on a completely different level.

No, instead he'd lost control completely, carried her upstairs and forced her to have sex with him.

That wasn't entirely true. If she'd really asked him to stop, he would have. But she hadn't. And that made things all the more puzzling. If she was still attracted to him, then they could build from there, couldn't they? Did they both have the courage to start over again?

He couldn't believe the direction his thoughts were taking him. He'd come to this house, followed her home from The Castaway, with revenge on his mind. Seeing her, getting her out of his system and walking out of her life. Finishing it once and for all. Now, after one night of lovemaking, he was already trying to figure out a way they could spend the rest of their lives together.

He was pathetic.

And still angry. Who the hell was this Arthur Beck and why in God's name did she think she wanted to marry him? That had been the part of the detective's report that had enraged him. She wouldn't marry *him*, but she'd marry this Beck guy, this engineer who seemed about as colorful as a stale piece of toast. Perhaps she'd finally decided to settle for security, but that couldn't possibly be true. Both he and Christy had learned early on that there was simply no such thing.

His arm was falling asleep, and he stretched it, trying to move as little as possible. He wanted to spend the morning in bed with her, and if it meant she had to be asleep, that was the way it went. As he glanced over the top of the woven bedspread—which he'd pulled over both of them in the middle of the night— he almost laughed out loud at the sight that greeted him. Several sleepy lumps of feline fur graced the bed: one calico, one Siamese, an orange marmalade tabby and a huge black cat.

Rutger's, of course. Mom Cat had shown up on the detective's report, the whole reason Christy was in this huge modern monstrosity of a house to begin with. He was proud of her, how well she'd done, while at the same time it had hurt to see her go on about her life so easily—and successfully—without him.

The only thing Jake knew he was sure of, as he watched the desert sunrise slowly filling the all-white, starkly modern bedroom with light, was that he'd handled things badly. He'd wanted to get Christy out of his system, and all that last night had revealed to him was that he was a long way from ever being able to let her go.

SHE WOKE to the knowledge that Jake was in bed with her.

Not Jake, she said, correcting herself. *A stranger. Not the boy you knew, but the man he's become. And you don't know this man.*

But you do, another voice whispered, a voice that was fueled more by instinct than common sense. *You know him in a way very few people know each other.* And that was true—each touch of his hand, the feel of his body against hers, the sound of his voice. It was as if she'd come alive again after a long period of feeling dead inside. The scent of his skin, the small scar on his forehead, the brilliant blue of his eyes. The way his mouth crooked slightly before he would let that full smile break through. The way that mouth felt on hers.

She let out a small sigh, then immediately regretted it because she sensed he was awake and now knew she was awake.

She felt his hand drift over her stomach, then slide up, beneath the fullness of her breast. He cupped it, squeezed gently, then plucked the nipple with the tips of his fingers.

She tried not to respond, even as she felt her body starting to melt.

He lifted her hair from the back of her neck with his other hand, then kissed the soft, sensitive skin there.

She closed her eyes.

"Turn around," he whispered.

She didn't really have any choice. Her body felt sore but oh so alive as she did as he asked. She studied his face again, having that same reaction that Jake was there, somewhere, behind this stranger's hard, closed expression. She endured his assessment of her, that long, lazy look from those blue eyes. Then she tensed as his hand, the one cupping her breast, moved lower. Between her thighs. Hot color flooded her face as she realized what her body was revealing to him.

He knew. He smiled. Eased her onto her back. Slid his body over hers. She almost started to cry, this was like so many mornings they'd spent together in Jake's apartment, beginning the day by making love.

She couldn't call this making love. It was more like making war.

He sheathed himself inside her with one sure thrust, watching her face as he did so. She closed her eyes, turned her head. He moved, and she caught her breath. He still had the power to affect her as no other man had—or ever would. It was a deep truth, and she wouldn't waste any time fighting it.

She couldn't deny him anything. She answered his determined thrusting with very sensual movements of her own, becoming lost in the sensation, almost on the brink, almost there, just about—

She felt his fingers twine into the strands of her hair and pull slightly. Her eyes opened, she looked up at him, so lost in an erotic, sensual haze.

"Does Arthur make you feel like this?"

His words were as effective as a bucket of ice-cold water, soaking her to the skin. Everything within her stilled, her desire extinguished completely. Even the cats woke with a start and jumped off the bed.

She struggled to get up, get him off her and outside her body, to reclaim a little space and time of her own.

"No," he said quietly, pinning her to the bed. "Answer the question."

Now she was furious, her breath coming in short, shallow spurts, her breasts rising and falling with exertion.

"What the hell do you know about Arthur!"

"Enough."

"Jake, it's none of your business—"

"You're my business. You've always been my business."

She turned her head away from the brilliance of his heated gaze. He was still lying on top of her, inside her. She lay beneath him, her legs apart, her body pressed into the soft mattress. Utterly and completely vulnerable.

"Why did you come here?" She asked the question on a sob, then bit her lip, forcing the next words out. "Why couldn't you just leave it alone?"

"I've tried. Christy, don't you think that if I could have left it, I would have?"

She knew he was telling her the truth, just as she knew it had been the same for her. Neither of them were over what they had been to each other. Neither had been able to move on.

"Just what are you planning to do?" She struggled a little more beneath him, but he held her still.

"I know you're alone here for the weekend. Three days, total. No one else is supposed to join you." He took a deep breath. "What I want—and what I think you owe me, after what you did—is some time with you."

She closed her eyes, not wanting to hear the rest, but knowing she had to.

"I want this weekend. I want to spend that time in bed and burn you out of my system. Then I want to be able to leave this house on Monday morning and never look back—"

"Jake, please—"

"No. I want to leave on Monday and be able to put you and what we had behind me. And I'm not leaving until you tell me why."

She'd known this moment was coming from the instant she'd lied to him, that long-ago night in the parking lot. But that lie had come from the deepest love she'd had for him, for the respect she'd had for his dreams. She hadn't meant to hurt him at the time. She'd meant to wound him so deeply that the cut would leave a scar. So that he would never want to have anything to do with her.

"I...can't do that." In retrospect, things had turned out tragically. How did that saying go, that hindsight was always twenty-twenty? But she'd been eighteen years old, and frightened. Immature. Unsure.

She'd done what she'd thought was best.

"Why not?"

"Because it's finished."

"Not to me." He lowered his head and took her lips with his, kissed her with such anger and strength and urgency that it stole her breath away. He slowly lifted his head and breathed the words against her lips.

"Not to me."

THEY SHOWERED together after they made love, and it infuriated her that he should feel he couldn't let her out of his sight. What was she going to do, bolt? Undoubtedly he knew her home address, and she wouldn't simply walk out on her responsibility to Rutger. Even if she'd left enough dry food for the cats, she didn't want to leave a house like this one all alone during a holiday weekend.

No, she'd have to talk Jake into leaving. He had to leave, before he found out why she'd broken off their relationship.

After their shower, they descended to the huge, modern kitchen. Jake helped her feed the cats, and she almost resented the action. It made him all the more accessible to her, not as much the avenging male. She didn't want to like him, and when she saw him encouraging the finicky Sasha to eat her food, emotion fluttered in her stomach.

"An omelet?" She held up a pan.

"Fine."

They were both silent while she cooked, and Christy couldn't help thinking of the irony of the entire situation. Here they were, in a million-dollar house, in its fabulous kitchen, both of them miserable. Further apart than they'd ever been, even in each other's thoughts. She couldn't stop comparing it to their earlier days, in Jake's small apartment, the kitchen with barely enough room for both of them. But those breakfasts—those breakfasts had been sublime. She knew she'd been deeply loved, and that she loved. Now, older and wiser by far, Christy knew what was important.

"You still like cheddar?"

He nodded his head.

"And ketchup with everything?"

He smiled, and she almost dropped the eggs. She knew he wasn't doing it deliberately; Jake had never really been aware of the effect he'd had on her. He'd simply loved her. And she knew he still had feelings for her, but not loving ones. The flip side of love was often hate, and he'd admitted to not being able to get past his relationship with her.

Maybe she could look on these few days together as a little bit of time out of time. Time they both needed to set things straight, get on with their lives.

Maybe they'd come to some sort of reconciliation . . .

She stopped that train of thought immediately, concentrated on the sizzling butter, then swirled the eggs into the pan. Jake simply sat at the kitchen table, looking through the windows at the mountains. One thing the house did have, though it was a bit too modern for her taste, was incredibly panoramic views of the desert, especially the mountains behind it.

She added the cheese, watched it melt, folded the cooked egg over, then slid it onto the platter she'd placed nearby. Toast popped up, she grabbed it and placed it on the same platter, then brought the whole lot of it toward the table.

Jake seemed to come out of his thoughts. "Juice."

"I'll get it—"

"Let me do something, Christy."

It was cruel, what he was doing. Countless times she'd wondered what it would have been like, to be with Jake now, to be reaching her thirties and have been with him all this time. To have shared breakfasts and dinners, nights in bed together, to have had all the time most married couples simply took for granted. *How was your day? What did you do? How are you feeling?*

It hadn't been meant to be.

They ate in silence, after Jake poured them both orange juice. Then, as she cleared away the dishes and Jake helped her wash up, she wondered what they were going to do for the rest of the day. Even the rest of the weekend. Theirs was not the sort of relationship that lent itself to questions such as, "So, how've you been?" or "What have you been up to in the intervening years?"

"Let's swim," Jake said suddenly.

"I didn't . . . I didn't bring a suit."

He simply looked at her. She lifted her chin a fraction.

"I wasn't expecting company."

"I didn't bring one, either, so we're even."

She didn't know what to say to that. Swimming in the nude with Jake didn't seem like such a smart idea, but he'd probably suggest the bedroom again, so what was the difference?

"Okay."

She could tell her answer surprised him, as she sauntered across the kitchen to the French doors opening out on to the pool.

He followed her, and she could feel his eyes on her as she shed her T-shirt and shorts. She hadn't bothered with shoes. Christy slipped off her underwear, then dived into the cool, blue water.

Her thoughts were scattered as she broke the surface. This was what she would have been doing here anyway. She'd planned these three days as a total rest. As a time of contemplation. In a way, having Jake here would simply speed up the process.

She looked up just as he dived in, and made sure to head for the opposite side of the pool. But he surprised her, not chasing her, making no attempts to seduce her. He stayed to one side of the giant, Olympic-size pool, swimming strongly, lap after lap. It made her tired just to watch him.

He didn't touch her the entire afternoon. Not when they got out of the pool and lay in the sun. Not when they went back into the water. She brought out some sandwiches and sodas for lunch, then they lay in the sun a little longer. By early afternoon, they'd retreated to the cool shade of the bedroom.

This time he let her take a shower alone, and Christy leaned up against the cool white marble of the stall, wondering how she was ever going to make it through the next few days if this one had just about done her in.

Her temples pounded with tension, her stomach was where she felt all her emotion and it was a tightly twisted mass of doubt and pain. How could Jake think this forced intimacy was good for either of them?

You could simply tell him what happened....

The thought was so tempting. He'd once been her best friend. She'd shared everything with him. But she didn't think he could ever forgive her for what she'd done, even if it had been done with the best intentions in the world.

She knew the exact moment he entered the bathroom.

"Are you planning on leaving any hot water for me?" His low, rough voice affected her as vividly as a caress, and her body stiffened, trying to ward off the feeling.

"I'm just about done." She tried for a brisk, no-nonsense tone.

"Want your hair washed?" He sounded almost playful and she gritted her teeth.

"No, thank you—"

He opened the shower stall door, and stood there. Looking at her. Admiring her. Though there was no reason to be afraid of him, Christy found herself averting her eyes as self-conscious color flooded her cheeks. She couldn't totally think of him as Jake—he still seemed such a stranger.

"I'll be done in a minute—"

"I just can't resist you," he said, closing the shower door behind him. "I never could."

She flashed him a look that she knew was filled with anger, then turned away. He had no right to play with her feelings this way, make her his plaything for the weekend. When he touched her shoulder, she flinched at the contact. He dropped his hand and she warily glanced over her shoulder.

"Why did you do it, Christy?"

There was no anger or accusation in his tone, nothing to make her afraid. It was as if she saw him with his guard down. She could tell that the fact that she'd flinched from his touch caused him tremendous pain. Jake had always been so full of life, with lively eyes and a ready smile. This man, standing both physically and emotionally naked in front of her, was so different.

"Jake," she began. She didn't know how to begin explaining what she'd done. "Jake, I always wanted you to go after your dreams—"

"But I didn't get the one dream I really wanted."

She stopped. He took her hand.

"To marry you. To be with you, have children with you."

Children. The word was her undoing. Tears filled her eyes and she turned her back on him again. This time, when he touched her shoulder, she didn't flinch.

She simply stood there, her head bowed, tears running down her face.

He gathered her into his arms, held her for a long time while she cried.

"I did what I thought was right." She forced the words out through her sobs.

"I know you did, Christy. But I have to know why."

"Please, please don't make me tell you."

"Okay. Okay. Not now."

He turned off the shower, then picked her up and lifted her out as if she were a child. He wrapped her in a towel, sat her on the side of the tub and carefully dried her hair. This was the old Jake, the Jake she'd loved, and it took every bit of emotional willpower she possessed not to start crying all over again.

He combed out her hair, then briskly dried himself. Knotting a bath towel around his waist, he knelt down beside her.

"I want to either let you go or start all over again."

She stared at him blankly, afraid to believe what she might have heard.

"Start . . . again?"

He smiled up at her, that familiar brightness in his eyes. "Why not? I've never met anyone that compared with you, and I don't think Arthur's the man for you."

"You'd . . . forgive me?"

He sighed, then looked down at the rug at their feet.

"I can't pretend to understand why you did what you did. But I can't see being unhappy for the rest of my life." His blue eyes blazed to life as he looked back up at her. "It's been hell without you, Christy. And I think if you're honest with me, you'll admit the same thing."

"It . . . has been. For me, too."

"So you'll at least consider it?"

She nodded her head, then glanced away, her emotions still turbulent, filled to overflowing.

She could feel his gaze on her, moving over her body as surely as if he'd touched her. He smoothed a strand of wet hair off her shoulder, and she instinctively moved toward his touch. She didn't want to fight with him. Not now, not ever again. She didn't want to cause him any more pain.

"Ah, hell," he said roughly, getting to his feet, unknotting the towel at his waist and letting it drop to the floor. "I don't give a damn if you never tell me anything. There's one way we know how to communicate and it's good enough for me."

With a swift, fluid motion he stripped the towel off her, then picked her up and carried her out of the bathroom toward the large bed.

HE MADE LOVE to her for hours in the shadowy bedroom, and when she finally fell asleep she was exhausted. Even as that exhaustion almost claimed her, she could feel his arm around her, his hand gripping her side, fingers biting into her sensitized flesh.

It's as if he's afraid I'll leave him . . . .

She knew then, without his ever having to put it into words, how the way she'd ended their relationship had affected him. She'd always been scared by the way she appeared in other people's eyes, what they saw and the opinions they formed of her—her drunken father, her disorganized family life. She'd placed such value on the opinions of a few high school students.

And she'd always thought about not being good enough for Jake. But she'd forgotten that the man lying beside her had lost both his parents at the age of twelve, had learned to live with that loss, and had given his sister the gift of a new life when he'd been merely sixteen.

Then she had been his family. And she had left him.

It was probably why they'd bonded to each other so strongly: neither of them had possessed families of their own. Jake had been alone, and she had been as good as alone. Then, once her father had died, she'd been truly on her own.

He shifted, and she knew he still wasn't asleep.

She turned so she was facing him, and put her head on his chest. His arms came around her and she remembered how many mornings they'd woken up this way, and how right it had seemed.

"A penny," he said softly.

"I was just thinking," she said, "how this has always felt perfectly right. You and no one else."

He tensed, and she wondered what he was thinking.

"Has there been anyone else?"

She thought of not telling him, then decided she didn't want any more lies between them.

"Two. Both were . . . awful. Because they weren't you."

He didn't say anything.

"You?" She had to know.

She felt his head move on the pillow, and he sighed.

"A few. A lot, actually. But no one who ever meant anything to me. I was a bit of a bastard, actually. I had a rule that I went by. One night, that was it. And no one ever got to spend the whole night." He paused. "I didn't want to wake up with them."

"How awful."

"Yeah, well, I wasn't that nice a guy in those days."

"Did it make you feel better, having that kind of control?"

"It was a hell of a lot better than the way you make me feel."

She propped herself up on one elbow, needing to see his face. And keeping the covers tightly around her.

"What does that mean?"

"Does it give you a sense of power, Christy, to know that you're the one person on earth who can make me lose control?"

She felt awful. "No. Not if it causes you this much pain." She placed a hand on his chest, needing to touch him. "Jake, if it makes you feel any better, you do the same thing to me."

"Obviously not that much or you would have come to Los Angeles with me."

They were back to that, even after he'd told her it didn't matter. She sighed, then lay down and pillowed her head on his chest. Funny what a person remembered. She'd always loved the way his chest hairs tickled her cheek. But she could also hear the rapid beating of his heart and knew he was still upset.

"Jake," she whispered.

"What?" He stroked her hair, and his touch soothed her as she drifted toward sleep.

"I'll go back with you. To Los Angeles."

"I could move out here for part of the time. I wouldn't want you to give up Mom Cat."

"I could do the same thing in L.A. The important thing is, I want to be with you. I know it's crazy, not seeing you all these years and then just deciding like this, but I haven't been happy since we broke up."

"Since you broke up with me. I never wanted to break things off."

"Since I broke up with you. I hope you'll forgive me, in time."

"I could forgive you a whole lot easier if I understood why." Her body tensed, and she knew he could feel it. "But I'm not going to let it get in the way of our being together."

She turned in his arms, took his chin in her fingertips and angled his mouth toward hers. Christy kissed him with every ounce of sweetness she could put into the kiss, then snuggled up against him. This was home. She could feel safe with Jake again. Probably in time she could tell him the entire story.

But for now, this was enough.

6

Thirteen years ago . . .

SHE WOKE up on the couch in Jake's living room, naked beneath the blanket, to the sound of the shower
running. Suddenly shy, Christy reached for her underwear, then her jeans and knit top. Once she was
dressed, she grabbed her backpack, ran a brush
through her hair, then pulled on her shoes.

By that time, Jake was finished with his shower.

She heard him leave the stall, then waited until he
entered the room. He had just his jeans on, and
reached for the shirt he'd discarded the night before.
She watched him as he buttoned it, again overcome
by this strange, sudden sense of unease.

This was Jake. Her Jake. Why did she feel so uneasy?

She knew it was because, in her heart of hearts, she
was worried that he still might consider her not good
enough for him. She was used to other people thinking that, but not Jake. Never Jake. She couldn't bear
it if he did.

"How are you feeling?" She could sense his gaze on
her, even though her head was averted.

"Strange."

He sat down on the couch with her, and took her hand. She turned to face him.

"I don't want to rush things, Christy. I don't want you to do anything you're not ready to do."

"Will I lose you?" That had been another fear she'd only given thought to late at night, in her bedroom at home.

"No. I can wait."

He took her home, gave her a quick kiss before dropping her off at the apartment complex she and her father shared. As she let herself inside, Christy realized that now it always depressed her to come home. It wasn't really a home after all. It was a place her father lived while he watched the small black-and-white television, waited for his disability check and occasionally ate a sandwich between drinks.

Now that television was droning softly as she stepped inside the door and closed it. Though it promised to be a scorcher today, her father hadn't turned on the air conditioner. The air smelled—the sour odor of liquor and cigarette smoke.

He was sprawled on his recliner, snoring, the ashtray on the small end table tipped over. Gray, powdery cigarette ashes were all over the olive shag carpeting. Several empty beer cans had been dropped on the floor around his favorite chair, along with a half-empty bottle of Johnnie Walker and the ever-present carton of cigarettes.

And it was as if she saw it through new eyes. The dirty carpet, smelling of the insect repellant she'd sprayed on it last summer. She'd meant to shampoo the hideous shag carpeting, but hadn't had time. The ugly plaid sofa, the dark green corduroy recliner, the grimy stucco walls, bare except for a cheap wall clock. The dingy ceiling, with little bits of glitter.

The ripple afghan, in a mound on the floor, the crocheted spread done in green, peach and cream. She'd made it for him one Christmas, only he'd passed out before they'd gotten around to opening their presents.

She set her backpack and books by the front door and went into the kitchen. Whatever she had to get done here, she wanted to get it over with. Both she and Jake had the day free, and she wanted to spend it with him.

The kitchen was a mess. Her father had obviously tried to make himself some sort of supper, completely disregarding the ham-and-cheese sandwich she'd left for him in the fridge, on a paper plate and wrapped in plastic wrap. How easy could you make dinner for someone?

The counter was littered with breadcrumbs, slices of bread, a mess that looked like part of a tomato and a half-opened package of salami. A jar of mayonnaise stood nearby, a butter knife sticking out of it, a large fly crawling along the sticky lid.

Ants were already making fast work of the bread.

She stood staring at it for a long time, and that all-pervasive fear took over. She'd never allowed Jake inside the home she shared with her father for long

periods of time, only once or twice. And timed carefully so they wouldn't stick around and her father had
a decent chance of being awake. But Jake had no idea
what he was really like, how much he actually drank,
how she constantly cleaned up after him. He was more
vegetable than man.

He'd hurt his back in an accident at work. She'd always secretly wished for a father with a more opti-
mistic attitude instead of the one she had. He'd simply
given up. If she were honest in her assessment of him,
she knew he'd given up shortly after her mother died.
There hadn't been a whole lot left to give to her.

She set to work, throwing away the wasted food,
cleaning the counter, putting a note on the refrigerator door to let him know that his dinner was still there
and good for this evening.

Christy tackled the living room, emptying the few
ashes left in the ashtray, then cleaning it, taking out
the small hand vacuum and collecting the spilled ashes
all over the carpet. She didn't worry about waking her
father, he could sleep through anything. She'd turned
on the air conditioner when she first came in, and now
draped the afghan around his legs in case he woke and
needed a little more warmth. Once the beer cans were
picked up and tossed in the trash, and the liquor bottle closed and placed in one of the kitchen cabinets,
her work for the day was finished.

She raced upstairs and showered. Once inside her
bedroom, she took a good look around and realized
how much of the little she owned was already at

Jake's. She'd moved it all over there in fits and starts, because they spent so much time together. Now, about all that was still in her bedroom was her school clothes, a few books, her cat, Boots, and the one picture she had of her and her mother together.

Someone had snapped it at a playground. She had to be about four years old. They were sitting at a nearby picnic table and her mother was smiling down at something Christy had in her hand. Something she was showing her. She still didn't know who had actually taken the picture. Now, as Christy stared at it, while wrapped in a towel, she picked it up. She couldn't remember the day at all. She didn't even know if her father had owned a camera back then, or if he'd taken the picture.

When she left with Jake early in the afternoon, she took the framed photo with her, slipped into her backpack.

THEY COULD HAVE DONE anything that day, her mind was totally on what was to come that night. She'd worn what she considered her sexiest lingerie, black lace, underneath the deceptive casualness of her jeans and light blue sweater. She'd done her hair a different way as well, in an intricate French braid she'd been practicing for a few days.

He noticed. Complimented her on it. She liked the fact that he did.

While they'd originally thought about going to a stable and checking out the horseback riding facilities, the hot weather put an end to that plan. Instead they took in a double feature, complete with a huge tub of buttered popcorn and two large Cokes. Afterward, they hung around the mall, did a little shopping. Christy picked up another, prettier frame for the picture she'd taken from home, then showed it to Jake as they headed back toward the car.

"She's pretty," he commented. "Do you miss her?"

"I don't really remember much. I wish I did."

"Your dad doesn't talk about her?"

She didn't want him to know. "I think it's painful for him, so . . . I respect his wishes."

They were in the car and leaving the mall when he asked her, "What now?"

She was feeling cocky. "I think you know what I want to do."

He grinned, then eased the car out of the large parking lot. "We should eat first."

"Well, eat a lot 'cause you're going to need lots of energy."

He simply laughed.

They went to Denny's. She had a secret soft spot, not for the chain itself, but for this particular coffee shop. She'd had her first cup of coffee with Jake here, had gotten to know him and decided she liked him. And all because of being frightened by what a few of her schoolmates had said in the bathroom.

Dusk had fallen, and though the only view from the large glass windows was of Highway 111, they could still see a little of the sunset against the mountains.

Night fell swiftly in the desert, much like the tropics, because the mountains surrounding the desert were so high.

They'd barely ordered when a policeman in the booth behind them got up and started for the glass double doors.

"Harry," an exasperated waitress called, "you've got to sit down and eat something. At least let me make your BLT to go."

"Can't," he called back, almost to the door. "There's a fire at the Lakewood apartment complex."

Everything within Christy stilled. Her father. Alone. *A fire . . .*

Then Jake was pulling her out of the booth toward the door, calling to their waitress. "Myrna, I'll be back to settle the bill. We've got to go."

THE HEAT was incredible, the flames roaring through the complex, sparks shooting up into the night sky. The entire west wing was in flames, and the apartment she shared with her father was in that west wing, on the ground floor.

As irrational as it was, she'd tried to run toward the front door.

"No!" Jake tackled her on the grass. Her face was hot from the heat thrown off by the flames, her tears felt hot, but she continued to struggle against Jake's hold.

"He's in there, he needs help—"

"Christy. Christy, if he was asleep in there, he's gone." She looked up into Jake's face, surprised to see tears welling in his eyes. "He's gone."

The shock was too great, she couldn't seem to assimilate it. "He must have gotten out, maybe he smelled the smoke, maybe—"

A fireman came up to both of them, motioned them back. Another came up beside them, and both Christy and Jake could overhear what they were saying.

"We're going to lose it, but it can be contained. Mac tried to get into that ground floor apartment, but it had already gone up."

"Aw damn, that tree's going to go any minute."

"And that cat."

Christy's head shot up, her gaze focused on the large grapefruit tree that had been close to their apartment. She'd seen it every day from the kitchen window. Boots, totally terrified, clung to several branches close to the top.

"Boots," she whispered, then struggled, tried to get out of Jake's grasp. She had to get Boots.

"Oh, no," the fireman suddenly in front of them said. "That tree's going to go up, and I can't have you going up with it. The cat will get away."

But Boots had been trapped in that tree before. He loved climbing up, racing along the limbs, digging in his claws. Yet he was a total moron when it came to climbing back down. Twice she'd had to call the fire department when he'd climbed too high for her to rescue him, and after that she'd decided he was an indoor cat. Her father must have let him out this evening.

"Hold on to her, okay?" Jake shoved her against the fireman, and with her body blocking him, darted away toward the citrus tree.

"Get back!"

"Crazy kid! He's going to get himself killed—"

"Jake!" She screamed his name, struggling against the fireman's hands, trying to get to Jake, if anything happened to him—

Though Jake had never had the time to give to school athletic programs, he moved like the natural athlete he was. She'd never seen anyone run that fast, or after reaching the bottom of a tree, climb so swiftly. Each handhold, each toehold, was accomplished within a minimum amount of time. Boots, still at the top, squalled even louder as the branches shook.

The fireman's voice was magnified over the bullhorn. "Get down, that tree's about to go!"

Jake was almost to Boots, struggling through the smaller, denser branches—

The top of the tree caught, the yellow-orange flames licking against the branches—

Boots's cries were now feline screams of terror—

"Aw, Christ!" one of the firemen muttered.

Then Jake grabbed Boots by the scruff, dragged the terrified cat off the branch—and jumped.

At the exact same instant, it was as if the tree exploded into flames. Jake tucked and rolled, coming up running, sparks showering him as he raced toward them, Boots clawing his chest.

He took Christy's arm as he passed her and practically dragged her to the Mustang. He got her into the passenger side, shut the door, then walked around to the driver's side, Boots clinging to him like an oversize burr.

Once inside the car, Jake unhooked the cat's claws from his shirt and let him go. He started climbing all around the back seat, crying and crying.

Christy stared at the apartment. Now the giant hoses, with their streams of water, were partially succeeding in putting out the flames. But it didn't really matter. She knew her father had been inside that apartment. The only time he ever really moved was to hand her his disability check and deposit slip. He used to accompany her to the supermarket, but that had been years before.

He had no other place to go.

She put her head in her hands and started to cry, felt Jake's hand on her shoulder. Then he was pulling her as close as he could across the front seat, cradling her in his arms, holding her tightly. Boots continued to squall in the back seat.

"He was in there, I know he was—"

"I know. Shh. I know—"

"If I'd been home—"

"There's nothing you could have done."

Boots howled, totally frightened now, in a strange car and sensing the fear around him.

"But if I'd tried harder—Boots, please be quiet!—
if I'd tried—"

"No. No. Oh, Christy, I'm so sorry."

HE DROVE HER BACK to his apartment, stopping at a
drugstore on the way to get a litter pan, litter and cat
food. Once they were home, Boots took up residence
inside the large bedroom closet, curled beneath a pile
of dirty laundry.

They sat out on the couch, and Jake opened a bottle of wine.

"This might help you sleep." They'd showered together, a first, as he'd had to help her stand. She'd
hated the smell of smoke, and he'd washed her hair so
gently, then her body, as she'd cried and cried.

She eyed the wine, thought of her father. And suddenly she had the clearest insight as to why a person
might drink. To simply stop the pain.

"Okay."

She downed one glass, not even tasting it, but soon
feeling its effect. Then she lay on the couch, her head
in Jake's lap, as he stroked her hair.

She took his hand, held it tightly.

"Talk to me, Christy."

"I'm scared." Her eyes welled with the tears that just
couldn't seem to stop falling. "I—I don't know what
to do. What's going to happen. I feel like . . . it's all
destroyed. I'm all destroyed. Inside."

"You loved him." He continued to stroke her hair.

She had loved him. Even in the midst of being frustrated and angry and ashamed, even despite the fact that on the day of his death she remembered wishing for a different sort of father, a braver one—she'd still loved him.

And now he was gone.

She gripped his hand harder. "Jake, please don't leave me." She hated the weakness she heard in her voice, but if something happened and she lost him on top of everything else, she knew she couldn't go on.

"Never." He stroked her cheek. "I'm going to sit here until you go to sleep, then I'm going to see what I can find out about what happened. Okay?"

"No, stay with me, please . . ."

"Just over the phone. I'm going to make a few calls."

"Okay. Okay." The wine, and the way he stroked her hair, the security of being close to him, all combined with her total exhaustion, and she slowly closed her eyes and finally slept.

AS SOON AS SHE was asleep, Jake called his boss, Bob.

"I won't be in for a few days. I can't leave her right now."

"I understand, Jake."

"But I don't want to screw up your schedule—"

"No, don't worry. This is a family emergency, I'll see if I can get Steve or Ned to cover for you. I'm sure they will when I tell them what happened." He paused. "Jake, I know a few of the guys over at the station. I can find out what happened. Do you want me to?"

"That would be a great help. You can call anytime, I'll be up. And Bob?"

"Yeah?"

"Thanks a lot."

BY MORNING, he knew exactly what had happened.

The fire had started in Christy's apartment. Apparently, from what the fire department's arson investigation unit could piece together, George Garrett had fallen asleep with a lit cigarette in his hand. He'd been too drunk to notice. His chair had caught fire first, then the apartment, then the entire west wing.

There wasn't a whole lot left of the body. The final identification had been made through his dental records.

Christy still slept. He'd moved her to his bed, and Boots had become sufficiently relaxed to come out of the closet and curl up on the pillow by her head. He still smelled of smoke, so Jake had taken him into the bathroom for a quick shampoo that, strangely enough, Boots had enjoyed.

Bob called again, around ten that morning.

"What does she want to do with her father's body?" He cleared his throat, obviously a little ill at ease. "I hate to ask at a time like this, but everyone knew George spent all his money on booze—"

Jake had suspected this. The few times he'd met Christy's father, the man had been nice enough, but the red-veined nose and cheeks, the sometimes vacant stare—it all added up.

"Have them take it . . . take him to Eiseley's Funeral Home. I'll make all the arrangements."

THEY WENT the next morning, and Christy had never hated an experience more than this one.

The funeral home director was a tiny little man who reminded her of a mole. He tried the standard spiel, but Jake quickly shot him down to size. His boss, Bob, had come with them, and Christy was grateful to both of them for helping her through such a terrible time.

Christy decided on cremation, then burial.

"But surely you want to give your father a funeral—"

Jake just gave him a look, and the director stopped talking in midsentence.

Christy took a deep breath. "He didn't have any friends. There isn't any family. He spent the last ten years of his life sitting in front of the TV. Drunk."

Jake had his arm around her, and now that arm squeezed her gently. She stopped talking, realizing she was dangerously out of control.

They picked the most modest arrangement possible, and still the fee quoted sounded immense to Christy's ears.

She took out her checkbook, her hands shaking. She had no idea where she'd come up with the rest of the money, but she would. "I can pay you part of it now, but the rest will have to wait—"

"But your young man has already taken care of everything."

Outside, they argued.

"I can't let you do this."

"It's already done."

"That was your money for Los Angeles."

"That was our money." He waved goodbye to Bob as they headed toward the Mustang.

She crossed her arms in front of her, hugging her middle, trying to keep back the feeling of intense pain.

"Then I'm nothing but a burden—"

"Stop it. Stop." He took hold of her upper arms and they stopped walking, right in the middle of the funeral home's parking lot. He looked down at her, and she'd never seen such a serious expression in those deep blue eyes.

"You'd do the same for me."

She nodded her head. "But it's never you. It's always me. Even when we met, you had to pull me out of that car, away from that jerk—"

His arms came around her, and he walked her to the side of the lot, beneath a stand of date palm trees.

"Listen to me. I want you to listen really hard. I need you to hear what I'm saying."

Her arms came down to her sides. She gave him the smallest, slightest nod.

"A lot of the things that went wrong in your life came about because you didn't have anyone protecting you. Am I right?"

Her eyes burning, she nodded her head.

"And a lot of what those people in school said was because you didn't let anyone get close because you were afraid of what they would see."

She felt so unbelievably tired. She nodded again, biting her lip against the strong emotion she felt rising inside her.

"But it wasn't your fault. None of it was your fault. I need you to believe this, Christy. I need you to get past it."

When she didn't answer, he rushed on.

"I can do anything in the world for you, and I want to, but none of it will work if you don't believe you're worth something. And that would mean more to me than anything else you could do."

"Why?" she whispered.

He tipped her chin up with one finger.

"Because I hate to see you hurting."

Her arms came up around him and she held fast.

"Your money—"

"It's money, Christy. I can make more."

"But you wanted to leave at the end of the school year."

"So I'll wait a year. So we'll leave after you graduate." Their original plan had included her attending her last year of high school in Los Angeles, but they wouldn't be leaving anytime soon.

"You're not mad?"

"No." He sighed, and tightened his hold around her. "I'm mad about the fact that you had to grow up the way you did. I'm mad that the fire happened. I'm mad that you had to be hurt. But mad about working for another year? It'll go fast. You'll see."

THEY FIXED SPAGHETTI that night, and Christy felt more at home with Jake than she ever had at her old apartment. That made the guilt come back in waves.

"I'm glad you didn't decide on a funeral," Jake said as they sat at the small table in the kitchen and ate their evening meal. "They're pretty awful."

"We would have been the only ones there."

"Bob would have come. And Steve and Ned and Ron."

"For you and me, not my dad."

"But that's what funerals are for."

She picked at her meal, and he noticed.

"Try to eat a little more."

She did, for him, not tasting anything. Afterward, they lay down on the couch and simply talked.

"Don't believe the people who tell you time heals it all, Christy. You remember for the rest of your life." Jake shifted on the couch, bringing her closer against him. "Hannah and I used to talk, after the plane crash. It's funny what people say to you, and I figured out years later that it's because they don't know what to say. They said to us, 'well at least you have each other.'"

"Oh, my God."

"Yeah, well, it's always astounded me that we can send a man to the moon, but we don't know how to talk to someone who's just been hit with a major tragedy."

"You know how."

He hugged her against his side. "I've always been able to talk to you."

They were silent until he felt the wetness of his shirt, her tears seeping through. He reached up over his head and handed her a wad of tissue from the box on the small side table.

"Thanks." She blew her nose. "All I do is cry."

"Cry all you want. Cry as much as you want. It's the only way to let it all out."

"You may regret saying that." She blew her nose again.

"Nah. Don't ever be embarrassed to cry in front of me."

She wiped her eyes, then put the soggy tissue on the coffee table. "How long did it take you to get over your mom?"

"I'm still getting over her."

"Tell me something about her. Something you remember. I can't remember much about my mother."

She felt his chest rise and fall with a long sigh. He was silent for so long she almost thought he wasn't going to answer.

"She was an artist."

"Really?"

"Oh, not a professional. But she drew. All the time. And she was really good, too. She did portraits of me and Hannah when we were little. I remember they hung in the hallway. She drew us all the time. Pencil sketches. Pastels."

"She was a dreamer, like you," Christy said quietly.

"Yeah. That's where I get it, because my father was as straight as they come. A businessman, but he wasn't real good with money. Neither was my mom. It was rough, the first few years Hannah took care of me, but she wouldn't give up. She didn't want us separated."

"You didn't have any relatives that could take you in?"

"Nope." He sighed again. "People talk a good line, but when it comes down to actually doing something, very few do."

She nodded her head.

"It's funny," Jake said softly. "I haven't thought about this in years. When I was little . . . she painted my room with rainbows. All over the walls. I used to love waking up in that room. Beautiful, all those colors, one blending into the next. My dad told me she worked on it for months while she was pregnant with me. She said she wanted me to have beautiful things in my life."

Christy remained perfectly silent. This was more than Jake had told her about himself in a long time. She'd never asked questions about his parents once she'd learned about the plane crash. It had seemed disrespectful of his feelings, somehow.

"She would have loved you."

"You think so?"

"I know so." He dropped a kiss on the top of her head. "She told me the same thing she said to my dad, that she wanted me to have rainbows in my life. Happiness. Love. I learned everything I know about love from her." He stroked her hair gently. "And I want the same for you. I want to give you rainbows."

"You already do."

They lay in silence, the apartment dark and quiet, content with each other. He continued to stroke her hair.

"It'll hurt like hell, Christy. For a long time. But I'll be here with you, and I'll help you get through it."

She moved, shifted her body so her lips were against his ear. "Would you do something for me now?"

"Anything."

"Would you make love to me?"

He didn't answer.

"Please, Jake. I want to feel alive, and I just feel so cold. I want . . . to be close to you that way."

He kissed her forehead, then got up off the couch, picked her up in his arms and carried her into his bedroom.

7

Friday evening, Memorial Day Weekend

SHE TOOK TWO STEAKS out of the freezer to defrost, then started rummaging in the produce bin for the makings of a salad. Jake found bread, and some pasta for a side dish. As they worked in the kitchen together, Christy couldn't get over the fact that, on one level, they seemed to have picked up where they left off.

She set out plates and cutlery at one of the small tables by the pool, even bringing out a fat candle in a brilliant blue glass globe, which she lit in defiance of the winds coming off the desert. It flickered, but held steady.

"It's pretty," Jake commented, coming up behind her. He wore just his black jeans, and looked sexier than any man had the right to. But he was completely unselfconscious with his state of partial undress, and of the effect he had on her.

She'd pulled on a pale turquoise dress, short, sleeveless, in gauzy cotton. Cool and uncomplicated. No underwear because of the heat. In deference to Jake's casual fashion statement, she'd left her sandals in the bedroom, and now the tile felt cool beneath her feet.

Once dinner was on the table, they spent the first few moments in silence, eating.

"It's very good," Jake commented.

"Thank you."

"You always were a good cook."

"You, too."

He ran a hand through his dark hair, rumpling it. But even disheveled, he was still a devilishly attractive man.

"You as nervous as I am?"

She hesitated for just an instant. "I can barely get my steak down."

"I'm going to go see if Rutger has any wine."

"Jake, wait!" She caught up with him in the kitchen. "Nothing from the cellar, but he put several bottles in the fridge he said I could choose from."

"Fine."

He selected one, opened it, then poured each of them a glass and set the bottle on the table.

"This is more like it. Relax, Christy."

"I'm trying. What do you want to do tonight?"

He smiled at her, raised an eyebrow.

"Besides the obvious," she said.

"I thought we might talk. Catch up with each other's lives."

"You seem to know everything there is to know about mine." After he'd mentioned Arthur Beck, Jake had admitted to the detective's report. That still rankled her.

"Touché. But what I don't know is even more important."

"What?"

"How you felt while you were doing what you did. What gave you the idea to start Mom Cat. What happened the first few years after I left."

This was leading to dangerous ground.

"That's true," she said, taking a careful sip of the white wine. She wasn't going to get relaxed enough to say anything that might trip her up later. But this evening could work two ways. There were a lot of things she still wanted to find out about Jake.

"Like twenty questions," she said.

"Yeah. Or truth or dare."

"Hmm." She thought about that. This could get interesting. "Okay. You first."

"Okay. Ask me anything."

She leaned forward, her chin in her hands. She took such great pleasure in simply watching him. No other man had ever affected her the way Jake did simply by being in the same room.

"What was the best part about being in L.A. that first year?"

He didn't hesitate. "Acting classes, and talking to all the other people who had the same sort of ambition."

"The worst?"

"Being without you."

Something stirred deep inside her. While many men played games, seemed to think it wasn't masculine to show true feelings, Jake had never bought into that. It was one of the things she'd loved most about him, how he shot straight from the hip emotionally.

He'd told her once that, after his parents were killed in the plane crash, he'd come to the realization that no one had all the time in the world, so why play games? What was so important about saving face, or holding on to one's pride? Why not say what was in your heart?

She wished she was as emotionally brave as he was.

"What's the most important thing you've ever learned and why?"

"Not to take anyone or anything for granted. And to not waste time." He hesitated. "Because of my parents."

Though their deaths had been terrible, Christy thought, Jake's mother and father had left him a powerful legacy.

And to not waste time. There. It was out in the open. The depth of his feeling for her was exposed by the fact that it had taken him twelve years to come back, and Jake had never believed in wasting time. She'd waited. She'd gone after him once, but turned back when she thought she'd seen the truth.

But what did anyone know at eighteen?

"Let's turn it around," he said suddenly, and she caught the determined gleam in his eyes. "What was the best thing about being out here that first year? After we broke up."

"There was no best thing. It was horrible."

"The worst?"

"Missing you. Feeling that I had done something irrevocably stupid. Wishing every single day that I had the power to turn back time." The words tumbled out and she realized that, with or without the wine's influence, these were thoughts she'd wanted to share with him for a long time. This conversation was long overdue.

He picked up his wineglass and took another sip. "And what's the most important thing you've ever learned in your life and why?"

"That pride is a poor substitute for love. I learned that when you left."

He stared at her for a moment, and she almost thought he was going to ask her to explain herself once again, why she'd broken up with him so long ago. But he didn't, simply turned his attention to his salad.

"You could have called at any time," he said, his voice low. "One phone call. That's all it would have taken."

The bite of pasta she had in her mouth was tasteless because she was so nervous. "It was a little more complicated than that."

"More complicated than the simple fact that we loved each other?" Now he was getting to the heart of it, and Christy knew he'd waited long enough. Before

Jake was through, before the weekend was over, he'd get to the bottom of it.

She lowered her head, all pretense of eating finished.

"Yes."

"You couldn't tell me."

"Of course not. It was all about you."

He took a deep breath. Another sip of wine. Leaned back in his chair. She could sense he was trying to regain some sort of control.

"How did you come up with Mom Cat?"

She was grateful for the reprieve. "I used to take care of customer's cats—the ones I met at the bar." She laughed self-consciously. "The customers, not the cats."

"I know."

"Anyway, the people I house-sat for said I took better care of their animals than anyone else they'd ever known. And I began to think about the area, how many people went off on business but still wanted their cats to be taken care of. I printed up a few fliers, word of mouth—the whole thing just grew."

"Boots would have been proud of you."

She thought of the little tabby she'd had as a teenager, with his grayish-brown tiger stripes and four white paws.

"He died last year. In his sleep." She blinked quickly, feeling her eyes sting at the thought of the little cat. "He still grabbed a nap in the laundry whenever he could."

"He was a good cat."

"I don't think I ever told you...how much it meant to me. What you did at the fire, when you climbed that tree."

He set his wine down, and she could see, from the expression on his face, that he was remembering.

"I was so mad that night. Everything you had was going up in flames, and I can remember thinking, I'll be damned if she's going to lose that goddamn cat!" He shook his head. "Don't ascribe heroic values to what I did, Christy. I was a pretty angry guy some of the time."

"Not with me."

"No. Never with you. How'd you get Sparky?"

She lifted an eyebrow. "How'd you know she was mine?"

He sighed. "The infamous detective's report."

"Oh. Well. I had a customer who never came home. After a few weeks, it was easier to move her into my apartment. She was so scared she lived in the bathroom sink, but now she's okay. Still easily spooked, but much better than she was."

"And the others are Rutger's."

"Yeah. I met him through Sasha." She told him the story briefly, then made another valiant attempt at her dinner.

"Your turn."

"Was it worth it?" she asked.

"Was what worth it?"

"The dream."

He sat back in his chair, the glass of wine in his hand, staring at her. "No."

"Why not?"

"Because there's nothing on this earth that could compensate for losing you."

So in a way, she'd been right. Jake would have given up all his dreams for her. She'd known it, as surely as she'd realized she couldn't do that to him.

"Then I was right to break up with you, because I don't think you'd have the same opinion if you'd never been able to try."

"That's bull."

"I don't think so."

"Was it really about that guy, Pete?"

She didn't want to lie anymore. "No."

"I never thought so." Something flickered in his eyes, the look he gave her was disquieting. "Were you pregnant?"

She hesitated for just a heartbeat. "No." That much, at least, was the truth. But now she wanted some answers. Their game took a highly emotional turn, and she was totally unaware of the direction they were headed. All she knew was that she had to know.

"And if I had been?"

"We would have worked it out," he answered.

"Meaning you never would have left town."

"No. Meaning we would have gotten married a little quicker than we'd planned, and shifted directions."

"Come on, Jake!" She sat back in her chair and glared at him. "I was eighteen, you'd just turned nineteen. The two of us, with a baby, wouldn't have stood a chance! Even if we'd made it to L.A., we never would have had the money for classes or books, the time for you to go on auditions, none of it. None of that best part you loved so much, talking to other people who shared your dreams. You would have ended up resenting me, I would have dragged you down—"

"Were you pregnant, Christy?"

"No!". She got up from the table and walked out on their half-finished dinner, into the kitchen, danger-ously out of control. He covered the short distance between them easily, grabbed her elbow and turned her, almost spinning her around.

"That was the reason, wasn't it?"

"No! Yes! I—"

"Damn it, Christy, don't lie to me! I need the truth!"

"I can't give it to you! Don't ask me to."

He jerked her against him, and she knew his anger had escalated. The breath rushed out of her as she made contact with the hard wall of his bare chest.

"Was there a child? Do we have a child?"

"No." She couldn't look at him. He forced her head up, made her meet his gaze.

"Did you have a baby? Is that why you made me leave?"

"No!"

"But you thought you were pregnant?" He had both her wrists in a punishing grip, and she couldn't twist away. She knew, with a shattering sense of finality, that this was where they were going to play it out to the end, that there was no turning back from this moment.

"Yes!" She twisted away from him and backed up, putting her hands out in front of her, warning him not to touch her. "Yes! I missed a period and I thought I was pregnant, so I went to the clinic and I—"

He stopped walking toward her, went perfectly still. And she saw, with terrible clarity, the pieces he was putting together.

"You were pregnant, so you sent me away, but you never had the baby..."

She couldn't have him believing that—she'd never have done anything to Jake's baby.

"No! *No!* Jake, I thought I was pregnant. I couldn't—I couldn't stand in the way of your dreams. You'd already given up so much for me, paying for my father's burial, waiting another year. I knew that if I told you I was pregnant, you would have stayed forever—"

"What the hell are you telling me!" He raked his hands through his hair, the expression in his eyes wild. Pained. "That you thought I would have abandoned you?"

"No! I knew you wouldn't, so that was why I sent you away, that was why I pretended to be in love with Pete, that's why I did what I did—"

He grabbed her wrist again, this time forcing her up against the pine table in the middle of the gleaming kitchen. She could feel it against her back, digging into her skin.

"Were you pregnant with my child?" The words were low, calm. So calm. She almost wished he'd yell at her, this was so much worse.

"No. I found out I wasn't after you left." Her voice broke on a sob. "But I wanted to be. If I had to give you up, I wanted your baby." She glanced up at him, saw the muscle working in his jaw. "The worst part after you left? Getting my period. Sitting in the bathroom and sobbing, knowing I'd been so cruel to you for absolutely no reason at all."

She could feel the emotion trembling through him. He'd wanted the truth, and now she wasn't sure he could handle it.

"That's it," he said.

Her throat closed. Jake was leaving her.

"Jake—"

"No. Don't say anything. *Don't.*"

She knew he was angry.

"How could you?" he whispered. He had her pinned up against the kitchen table, an arm on either side of her, his body pressed to hers. "How could you make a decision like that without telling me the truth?"

Her stomach was quivering so badly she could barely form a coherent sentence. "I thought that what I did was . . . for the best."

He stood still for a long moment, and time stretched to the point where Christy thought he would finally step away from her and walk out the door.

"Why did you stop loving me?"

That one question broke her heart.

"I never did. I wanted you to . . . be happy."

He simply shook his head, as if he were still dazed by the strength of her revelations. Then he leaned forward, head bent, touching his forehead to hers.

"Why did you stop believing in me?"

"Oh, Jake, I never did."

"Yes, you did. You thought I couldn't care for you. You didn't believe I could support you—"

"But not at the expense of your dreams," she whispered. Now, in his arms, she could see how wrong her decision had been. She'd been eighteen, and frightened, and hadn't known what to do. She hadn't felt she was of worth to him, and she'd sent him out of her life.

"To hell with my dreams!" Now he caught her face in his hands, forced her to look up at him. "Do you think I consider myself some big success, because I went to Los Angeles and took a few acting classes? Sure, I've done a lot of movies, and I make a decent living, but do you honestly think I believe I'm a success?"

She didn't know what to say.

"The other night, before I left to come out here, I was at the market. And I saw this guy, and his wife. She was pregnant, and the way she looked up at him, the way he was with her—*that's* success. *That's* more of a success than any amount of fame, or any goddamn movie I could have made. Because if you don't have that, you don't have anything. And the only person I ever wanted to share that part of my life with was you, Christy. *You*."

She'd known this anger was inside him, had known from the first moment he'd grabbed her arm out by the pool. And he was right about losing control around her. She couldn't move because he was pressed up against her, and she knew she had to ride this storm out no matter how his words hurt.

"Do you think I'm proud of the way I've lived my life since we broke up? It's pathetic, sending women away after we've screwed our brains out, or going back to their place and leaving right afterward. But I didn't want anyone else. Damn it, Christy, even in the middle of it, all I could think of was you, the way we were together, the way you were, how much I loved you—"

The pain was washing over her in waves, great waves that knocked all the air out of her, that practically shut down her breathing. There had been times, right after the breakup, when she'd tried to console herself with the fact that Jake had probably met up with some sharp actress in Los Angeles, someone who was far more capable than she was of helping him get what he wanted.

But all he'd wanted was her. And she'd made a disastrous decision, completely based on fear.

"You were wrong. You were *wrong*, Christy, you had no right to do what you did! How the hell did you know how I'd react to the fact that you thought you were pregnant? Why couldn't you have even considered I might have been *happy* about it? That we could have built something even stronger than we already had? We loved each other so much—Christy, why didn't you believe there was enough love for a baby?"

This was a pain beyond tears. She was numb inside, seeing for the first time that she'd denied Jake so much, caused him such emotional agony.

She tried to twist away from him, unsure if she could bear any more of this.

"No." He backed away from her, let her go. They weren't touching at all; he had no hold on her. He simply held her gaze with his own.

"Don't you walk away from me. Not now. We're finishing this."

She knew he was right, but she was terrified of this man. He could destroy her. Not physically—he'd never hurt her that way. But emotionally. She was finally, on a deeply heartfelt level, seeing what the consequences of her decision had been, and once again realizing how inadequate she was.

If she'd had one other person to talk to about her decision, even a distant member of her family. A girlfriend. A counselor. But she hadn't been a girl who trusted easily, and Jake had been everything to her then. Yet Jake had been the one person at that time she couldn't talk to, could never tell the truth to.

"I didn't want to hurt you." The whispered words sounded loud in the quiet kitchen.

He threw back his head and laughed. The sound chilled her. She rubbed her upper arms, suddenly cold. So cold.

"You didn't want to hurt me." He was pacing the kitchen now, back and forth, then he glanced at her. "You didn't want to hurt me."

Suddenly he turned and slammed his fist into the wall. She jumped at the swift action, her heart in her throat.

"You tore my *heart* out, Christy!" He cornered her then, slapping both hands down on the table, on either side of her. Trapping her.

"I was eighteen, Jake—"

"I don't care."

"I did what I thought—"

"Yeah. Right."

She realized he was in such pain he couldn't hear a word she was saying. Didn't want to. This was what he'd come to her for, this emotional purge. And she wondered if things would ever be the same between them again.

"I didn't mean—"

"To hurt me. I know. You did. You didn't trust me, Christy. You didn't believe in me. Well, I want you to know something."

She couldn't look away from the anger in his blue eyes.

"I never would have left you. Never."

She swallowed.

"And right up until the end, when you sent me away? I trusted you. With everything. My heart, my life—" He stopped then, and it was as if he'd suddenly run out of words. There was nothing left to say.

Silence. She held her breath, waiting for him to walk back to the bedroom, pull on the rest of his clothes, grab his keys and head out into the desert night.

He'd gotten what he wanted. The truth. The reason she'd broken off their relationship. And she was so afraid that he'd never be able to see beyond what she'd done. He'd never be able to forgive her.

Yet she knew he'd carried this burden for twelve years. Jake needed some time to be angry. She'd carried the truth for such a long time, but at least she'd known why it had to happen. Now, despite the fact that it was twelve years later, she knew this man. Felt for him. He'd never hurt her. He'd come here seeking understanding. And he was caught in the middle of it. Trying to get through it. Reaching for transcendence.

"Jake?" she said. Her voice was tentative.

"No. Don't say anything. Just . . . wait."

She did, feeling the tension in him, the immense self-control he was imposing. She waited, hoping he could sense just a little of the love she felt for him, even at this terrible time.

"Okay," said Jake. "This is the way it's going to be."

She stilled. Hoping. Praying. *Please don't let him leave me. . . .*

"You're going back with me. To L.A."

She let out her breath.

"We're getting married."

She didn't move. Couldn't.

"And I'm getting you pregnant this weekend."

Her head shot up. She started to say something, and he simply placed a finger over her lips.

"No. *No.* Nothing you can say is going to make me change my mind. We've wasted enough time. Do you know, Christy, we could have had a couple of kids by now?"

She'd thought about it all the time.

"I'm taking control of things because I can't trust you to make any kind of decision—"

"Jake, wait—"

"No. You either trust me or you don't. You either want to be with me or you don't. There's no in between this time, Christy. There can't be." His large hands were sliding up beneath the short skirt of her dress, finding nothing to impede them in their search. He found her, the heart of her, then slid his hands around behind, grasped her bottom, lifted her up so she sat on the edge of the table.

"Jake, I—"

His arm shot out behind her, knocking several bowls, knives and half a head of lettuce off the table. Then he was bending her back, following her down.

"Are you using anything? The pill?"

She shook her head.

"I hope you're feeling fertile." He was working the fastening of his black jeans, never taking his eyes from her flushed face.

She knew better than to argue with him.

He grasped the front of her blue gauze dress, right at the neckline, then jerked down. The material gave way, and he parted it, looking at her breasts. Her breath was caught short, erratic. He lowered his head and kissed the pulse beating frantically at her throat.

"It's really simple," he said, working his way down her body, then taking a nipple between his fingers and rolling it, so slowly, so gently, until it hardened into painful awareness. "You're going to give me back what you took from me."

She didn't know why or how, but suddenly she saw beyond his actions to the emotion beneath. Fear. He was trying to conquer her, control her, because at the deepest level of his being he was afraid she was going to leave him again. The thought flashed into consciousness so easily, felt so very right. He might act as if he were in control, as if he were merely toying with her, but Christy knew Jake was feeling frustrated by his lack of control. Over his emotions. Over the relationship. And over the past.

What had Keith told her that evening at the bar? That people basically acted from one of two emotional bases. Love or fear. There was nothing else. Love joined together, where fear ultimately separated and led to loneliness and pain.

She'd been separated from Jake long enough. They'd both been through enough. It was time for her to start loving him the way she'd wanted to, so long ago. If fear hadn't gotten in the way.

She touched his hair, ran her fingers through the soft, thick strands. He stilled, then reached up to remove her hand.

Close, but not too close. He wouldn't allow it.

But she was going to break through to him.

When he tried to take her hand in his, remove it, she stiffened her arm. Wouldn't let him move her fingers. He stared at her for a long moment, then eased his hold.

She didn't look away from him as her hand moved to the side of his face, cupping his cheek, then tracing the strong line of his jaw. Words wouldn't have done any good right now, her actions were suffused with her love for him, told him more eloquently than simple speech ever could what he had always meant to her. Time apart, space and distance had no meaning for them. They'd always loved each other, always been in the other's thoughts. And hearts.

His hand on her breast stilled, the blatantly sexual touch meant to distance him from her ceasing. His hand moved to her side, and he simply held her as she touched his face, looked into his eyes. Her heart felt so full, and she tried to put all that feeling into her eyes, her touch, to tell him how sorry she was. How she wished she'd never made the decision that had torn them apart. How she wished she'd never doubted their love, given it over to the intense fears that had torn her apart.

She tugged his hair, at the same time raising her upper body off the hard wood of the table. Offering herself for his kiss, his touch. Wanting to be of comfort to him, wanting him to use her in any way he wished if it would ease his emotional torment. It was all in her body language, her eyes, the way she touched him.

He didn't say a word, merely lowered his head until their lips met. She saw the look in his eyes before she closed her own, saw the brilliant sheen of tears in his.

Love or fear, Keith had said. *It's always your own choice.*

She chose love, feeling his arms around her waist as he lifted her from the table, winding her arms and legs around his strong body as he headed toward the stairs. And knowing that this time it would be different. Not in anger, or in rage, or to satiate a sexual hunger that burned so brightly it threatened to obliterate all sanity.

This time, what they would find in that cool shadowy bedroom would be healing. A measure of peace.

This time, it would be love.

8

Twelve years ago . . .

CHRISTY STOOD next to the pay phone at the drugstore, the receiver in her hand. Waiting. Hoping.
Praying. Jake was at work. She wasn't due to see him
until she picked him up tonight. She was on her break
that afternoon, and had called the family planning
clinic exactly at the time the nurse had told her to.

"Mrs. Landes?" She hadn't given them her real
name. She'd told them she was married, and Jake's
promise ring had almost made the lie a truth.

"Yes?" Christy said, biting her nail. *Please God,
please, don't let it be true. . . .*

"Congratulations. You're pregnant."

"HEY, YOU." Jake swung into the passenger seat, his
eyes alight, that restless energy she loved in full com-
mand of his actions. He kissed her, then sat back as
she turned on the ignition.

"Hey, yourself." Her mind was going a thousand
miles a minute. More than anything, she simply
wanted to go home, ask Jake to hold her and tell him
the truth. She'd missed her period, she was over ten
days late. Christy hadn't wanted to chance this to a

home pregnancy test, because she'd heard some of the brands were unreliable. So she'd gone to the clinic under an assumed name. And gotten an accurate test.

Now she couldn't bear to tell him. For she knew it would be the end of every dream Jake had ever had.

Dinner was already in the Crock-Pot when they got home. Chili. She whipped up some corn bread and popped it into the oven while Jake took a quick shower. Then he joined her in the kitchen.

"Look what I got." He spread a handful of maps on the small table, then sat down on one of the chairs. "I stopped by Triple A this morning. I don't know why, it's just east on the 10 almost the entire way, but it makes it seem more like a trip."

She was quiet, ladling chili into two bowls, cutting the corn bread, getting out the salad.

"One more week and we're out of here."

She'd graduated a few days ago, and Jake had been the one cheering her on in the audience. She hadn't thought of her father being in attendance, because even if he'd still been alive, he probably wouldn't have made it.

Christy had even gone to one of the guidance counselors, to see if she could figure out some sort of dream for herself. Not as big as Jake's. Never as big as Jake's. She wasn't out to change the world, just to find her own little corner of it. She'd taken a few of the tests, and all that had been revealed to her was that she was essentially a people-oriented person. And she'd already known that. Sometimes she had a feeling that,

given a chance, she would have been much more so-
cial than she was. Her shyness came more from lack
of actual practice with people, not from a feeling that
overwhelmed her.

"I picked up a lot of fliers about what to do once we
get there. We can go to Malibu, and Universal Studios. I'd kind of like to drive down to Disneyland—"

She set a bowl of chili in front of Jake, and the plate
of corn bread. She listened while he talked about the
trip, wondering how she'd ever be able to tell him.

Oh, by the way, I ruined your dream. . . .

She wasn't sure when it had happened. Jake was
always scrupulously careful about their birth control. The foam had given her a rash, painful and red
on the inside of her thighs. Changing brands hadn't
helped the problem. But they'd always used condoms. Every time.

She pushed her chili around in her bowl while she
listened to him make plans, spin dreams for both of
them. And thought about how, except for her pregnancy, she would have been so excited, looking forward to this change, knowing that they were on their
way to a brand-new life.

Now she sat. Outwardly calm, inwardly sick,
trembling and tense. Frightened. Not knowing what
to do.

They made love that night. As she clung to him in
the darkness, her throat aching with the need to con-
fess, the seeds of a half-formed plan began to take root
in the darkest, most fearful corners of her mind.

THE DAY they were due to leave, she broke up with him.

Everything was packed and ready. They'd talked to the landlord, arranged for the phone to be disconnected, made sure Boots had his bath and shots, both their cars were packed full. Jake had bought her a used Volkswagen Beetle for her eighteenth birthday, with a bright orange paint job. He hadn't liked the color, but she'd told him she loved it, and she did. She called the car her little firefly, and had thought of their future in Los Angeles. He'd be in the Mustang, going to auditions. She'd be in her Bug, going to the grocery store or maybe taking a class at a local university.

She wanted him to be proud of her. She didn't want to hold him back. If Jake became famous and they were invited to fabulous parties with international stars, she'd have to be able to talk to them, wouldn't she? More than anything, she didn't want to embarrass him.

Now she had. In the back of her mind, she'd never shaken the label of bad girl. Fast. Easy. It didn't matter that she'd been a virgin when she and Jake had first made love. It didn't matter that she'd only been with him. Bad girls, lower class girls, they were the stupid ones. The ones who got pregnant. The ones who got caught.

She never gave a thought to the idea that it took two people to create a child. Jake hadn't wanted children. He wanted a career. He'd always been careful to use condoms. She'd been the one, so eager to make love, wanting to rush to that burning, passionate culmination, who wouldn't have known if he'd been wearing one or not.

And probably wouldn't have cared.

While they were packing, she made sure that all of her things were in the little orange Volkswagen. There was even room for Boots in his carrier. She'd thought about sitting down and just carefully explaining to Jake that she didn't love him anymore, but at the last minute her courage failed her. While he went to the station to pick up his final paycheck, she wrote him a note. It was pathetically inadequate, but it would do the job.

Jake, I can't go with you. I'm sorry.

SHE DROVE the Volkswagen, with Boots squalling inside, as far out of town as she could. Got off the freeway. Drove north to an unfamiliar town and simply sat in the car, in a supermarket parking lot. Waited. He'd go on. He had to.

Right around midnight, she headed home.

She stopped at Denny's to use the bathroom. Staring at herself in the mirror, she got out her makeup bag and lined her eyes. Put on a heavier coat of lipstick. Survival was the order of the day, and she'd need someone to look after her until the baby was born. Pete Wilford had never made any secret of the fact that he liked her. He was a biker, but he was okay. Not as bad as the others.

You finally found your own level.

She slammed her makeup bag into her purse and headed out into the night.

HE FOUND HER when he saw her car in the Circle K parking lot. Jake turned the Mustang into the lot behind the store, then walked toward the front.

She was sitting behind Pete on his motorcycle when she heard Jake's voice.

"Christy."

She turned her head. He was standing in the front parking lot, less than ten feet away from her. Funny how it should end here, when it had all started here. He'd pulled her away from Rick almost two years ago, and now she was going to make sure he left her with Pete.

"Yeah?" She desperately tried to inject an uncaring note into her voice.

"What is this?"

She would have felt better if he'd yelled at her. Cursed. Called her names or assigned blame. But he just looked at her, asking her to explain. His body was tense. He had himself under control, but she could see the uneasiness, the pain, in those dark blue eyes.

"You got the note." She turned back toward Pete. He handed her his bottle of beer and she took a small swallow. Normally she hated the stuff, but she wanted Jake to see that she was with Pete now. Sharing everything.

"Can we talk—"

"Hey." Pete was in a gloriously macho mood, flexing his muscles, showing off the large tattoo of an eagle on his right bicep. He looked like a muscle-bound Frank Zappa, with long stringy black hair held back with a red bandanna. The girl he'd always had the hots for was on his bike, and it was clear he finally saw himself in the running. But Christy knew he didn't want her heart or her mind. Her body was more than enough. "She doesn't want you."

Jake was silent for a moment. When he finally spoke, his voice was quiet. Controlled. "I'd like to hear that from Christy, if it's all right with you."

She owed him that much. She'd have to do it quick, move in for the kill, get him to leave before she gave in and begged him to take her with him, baby and all.

"Fine." She got off the bike, making sure she showed a lot of leg. Cheap. Slutty. She sauntered over to him as if she didn't have a care in the world, while all the time her heart was breaking.

"Christy." He walked with her a little way, in order to distance them from Pete and his group. "What's wrong?"

"Nothing. I just—when it came time to go, I just—changed my mind."

"Do you want to stay here? Is that it? I could—"

"No. That's not it."

He ran his fingers through his hair. Stumped. He glanced away, and she had that same feeling he was fighting for control.

"Baby, if it's something I've done—"

"It's nothing you've done. Nothing. Get that through your head. We just want different things."

"I thought you wanted to come with me—"

And then she knew how to push him away, so far away he'd never want to come back.

"It's stupid, Jake. The whole idea. How the hell are you supposed to become an actor?" She laughed, twisting her face into a semblance of a smile. "I only went along with the whole thing because I didn't think you'd ever have the guts to truly do it. But now that you're ready to go, well, I'm not."

Fighting down the nausea in her throat, she turned her head and looked at Pete with what she hoped was longing.

"I'll be there in a minute, babe."

He grabbed her arm, forced her to face him.

"What the hell is wrong with you?"

She had to get away from him, couldn't let him touch her, change her mind. "Nothing! This is the real me, Jake, so you'd better get used to it."

He reached out, took his finger, smeared some of the heavy cream blush on her cheek.

"Come back with me. Come on, Christy. We'll get a hotel room. We won't leave tonight. We can talk about what you want." He cleared his throat, and she could see the desperation in his eyes. It was killing her.

"Maybe I didn't pay enough attention to what you wanted. Maybe it was always about me. But I didn't mean it that way, Christy. I always wanted you to be a part of it."

"Yeah? Well, I don't." She backed away from him, the heels of her black boots shaky in the gravel. "Get it through your head, Jake. I don't love you. I never—"

She couldn't say it, it was too horrible a lie.

"I used to, but I don't anymore. I don't love you! I don't want to go anywhere with you, ever!"

She turned and walked toward the group. Jake followed.

"Hey," Pete said, enjoying the sight of this immensely. "She said she didn't want you anymore, grease monkey."

Jake ignored him, grabbing her arm again, spinning her around to face him.

"Damn it, Christy, tell me the truth. What's going on?"

"Leave her alone." Now Pete was getting off his motorcycle, and several of his friends were doing the same.

"I don't have any quarrel with you, man. I want to talk to Christy. This is none of your business."

"If it has to do with her," Pete said, flexing his muscles again, "I make it my business. Now get back in your car, faggot, and go on out to Hollywood where you belong."

Jake ignored him. "Christy, listen to me—"

Two of Pete's friends caught Jake from behind, holding his arms. He exploded into action, struggling against their hold, but not before Pete slammed his fist into the side of his face, splitting his lip.

"No!" Christy screamed, launching herself at Pete, trying to stop the attack. She'd never meant for this to happen.

They let him go, and Jake staggered back, wiping his hand across his mouth, staring at her as if he didn't recognize her. For one agonized moment, she considered telling him the truth. But she knew she couldn't.

She picked up a handful of coarse gravel from the parking lot and threw it at him. "Go! Get out! Get away from me!" She threw another handful. "I hate you!"

He stood there, blood on his face. Hesitating.

She pulled the friendship ring off her finger, and threw it at him. "And take your stupid little diamond! I never want to see you again!"

He didn't move, simply stared at her.

She wasn't going to be able to pull this off unless he left. The longer he stood there, the weaker she became. So she swallowed against the tightness in her throat and said the one thing she didn't think Jake would ever be able to forgive her for.

"I've been seeing Pete for months. While you were at the station, working those double shifts. I got lonely. I hated that goddamn dream! I hate you, Jake! I really hate you—"

That made him move. Her vision blurred with tears as she saw him wheel around, walk off, his back ramrod stiff. She hurt for every step he took.

"Boy, that's telling him, Christy." Pete took another swig of his beer, turned to his buddies and laughed.

JAKE DROVE NONSTOP to Los Angeles that night, and checked himself into the first motel he found, on Sunset. Then he went to the liquor store on the corner and got two six-packs of beer, went to bed and found blessed oblivion.

"HERE WE ARE." Pete unlocked the front door of his apartment. Christy followed him inside, carrying Boots in his case.

"Let me just fix a litter box for him."

He kept staring at her breasts. She knew the price she'd pay for spending the night at his place, but it didn't matter. Nothing mattered. She'd carry the look on Jake's bloodied face to her grave.

Once Boots was settled—in Pete's front closet, this time—she knew she couldn't stall any longer.

"Hey, babe." He patted the couch next to him. "Let's get comfortable."

"Okay." He'd had a lot to drink tonight. For all she knew, he might not even be able to perform. That would be a relief.

She saw no reason to play games, and sat close to him on the couch. Pete didn't waste any time. He pulled her against him and kissed her. His mouth tasted like a cross between an ashtray and a can of beer. She grimaced, but he was really into it, his hands everywhere, sticking his tongue all the way down her throat. She fought the urge to gag.

He broke the kiss. "Lord, you're sweet. Let's get that top off and have a look."

The sooner she got this over with, the better. She stood up, numb, then peeled her black T-shirt over her head. She unsnapped the black bra beneath it, then slid it off.

He stared, one happy man. "God, you're gorgeous. Come here."

She still had her boots and short skirt on. He took her hand and pulled so she was standing in front of him as he sat on the couch. Then he eased her down so she was straddling his thighs.

"Oh, yeah," he breathed as he touched her. Shaped and fondled her. He couldn't get enough. Within seconds, his head lowered and he was mouthing her breasts.

She felt absolutely nothing. Not even revulsion. She was cold, from the top of her head to the tips of her toes. And the only thing that kept her from screaming and running out of the apartment was the knowledge that she carried Jake's child. She would keep a part of him. And she would do anything she had to to survive.

He eased her down on the couch. Covered her with his body. When his hands touched her panties, she flinched.

He didn't even notice.

Then he unzipped his pants and she saw his erection. It looked huge and red and ugly, and she knew she could never live with herself if she let him put it inside her.

"Oh, God!" She rolled up off the couch and sat on the far end of it, shaking. Shaking so violently she thought she was about to be sick.

"Christy?" Pete was still on his hands and knees on the couch; she'd scooted right out from under him.

"Wait. Please wait a minute. It's going too fast—"

"Sure. Sure." But it was clear Pete didn't have a clue as to what was going on. Still, he zipped his pants up, lit a cigarette and offered her one.

She burst into tears.

"Hey! Hey, okay, we can go slow, Christy. I guess I shouldn't have just jumped your bones, but when you told Jake we'd been getting it on for months, hell, I thought you had the hots for me."

That made her cry even harder.

She could see the beginning of comprehension dawn in Pete's expression. "You love the guy."

She nodded her head, reaching for her T-shirt. She slipped it on, then crossed her arms in front of her waist, hugging herself.

"What the hell did you—what was all that in the parking lot?" He seemed as uneasy with a crying woman as he would have been with a live grenade. But he did hand her a box of tissues.

Between sobs, she told him everything. Under normal circumstances, Pete Wilford, biker, wasn't the person she would have chosen to spill her guts to. But he was there. And he proved to be a total surprise.

"Aw, damn." Now he had his arm around her, and was awkwardly patting the top of her head. "Same thing happened to my sister, only the guy was a real bastard and wouldn't have anything to do with her."

She blew her nose, then caught her breath on another soft sob.

"Hey, it's okay. Pregnant women cry a lot. I know."

"I'm sorry—"

"Hey." He spread his fingers, palms out in front of him. "It's okay."

"I don't know what to do—"

"You can spend the night here—I won't touch you, you know that. And in the morning I'll take you to see my sister. You need to talk to another woman."

She nodded her head. "I guess so."

"God. Tough luck. Why couldn't you tell him?"

She told Pete why, all about Jake's dreams and what they'd planned.

He thought about this as he ordered a takeout pepperoni pizza and a six-pack of beer. "You want soda?"

She nodded her head again.

She managed to eat a slice while Pete made short work of the rest. He wasn't at all fat, and she wondered where he put it.

"I think you're making a big mistake."

She glanced over at him. Christy felt so tired, she could have almost passed out on the couch. This would go down in her personal history as — easily — the worst day of her life.

"You do?"

"Yep. If I was Jake, I'd be proud to have a woman like you carrying my kid."

"But . . ." She told him about her father, about the fire. The way Jake handled all the bills. The way he'd had to defer his dream for a year.

"I knew your old man . . . he used to come into the liquor store near Monterey and Highway 111. He was a nice guy. I was sorry to hear about that fire, Christy. I looked in the papers for funeral services, but couldn't find them."

She didn't know what to say. She never would have thought of Pete as the sort of man who was revealing himself to her tonight.

"And another thing, Christy. A man likes to feel that he can take care of his woman, you know what I mean? I bet it made Jake feel really good that he could do something like pay for your old man's burial. You needed him and he could come through for you, you know?"

Pete was making a strange kind of sense. She'd never thought of it from a man's point of view.

He must have seen the expression on her face. "Hey. I know what people think of me, but I'm no animal. Christy, I thought you wanted to . . . you know . . ."

"It's okay, Pete. Thanks for backing off." She thought of Rick, of most of the boys she'd known in high school before Jake, and was thankful Pete was nothing like any of them. In his own bizarre way, he reminded her of Jake. She could almost—not quite—forgive him for hitting Jake.

"Look," Pete said, between mouthfuls of pizza. Boots must have smelled the fragrant pie because he was peeking around the living room door, his whiskers twitching. Pete threw the cat a slice of pepperoni. "I'll drive you to Los Angeles, if you want. Tell him, Christy. I bet he'll be the happiest man in the world, to hear about that little bambino. Hell, if he's not, I'll drive you back and you can stay with me."

She gave him a look.

"Just friends, okay?"

That alternative, even though it was similar to the one she'd planned, still surprised her.

"You wouldn't mind if I was pregnant with another man's child? And no sex?"

"Like I said, you're a good-looking broad." He picked up another slice of pizza, took a bite, swallowed. "It'd give me status, so long as the guys didn't know we weren't fooling around."

She nodded, seeing things from his perspective. Male pride.

"Now, don't take this the wrong way, Christy, but that was a little taste of heaven you gave me on this couch."

She flushed, could feel the color racing up her neck.

"I'm sorry. I thought I could do it, Pete—"

"Yeah, I know. But not when you love another guy."

SHE STOPPED by the Circle K the next morning and hunted around in the parking lot until she found the promise ring. She slipped it on to the thin gold chain around her neck, and just having it there, with Jake's class ring, made her feel better.

Christy dropped in at the family planning clinic three days later to pay the remainder of her bill. Normally she would have paid the entire amount up front, but she hadn't wanted Jake to know about the test and had had to sneak the money out of their grocery fund.

"Oh, Mrs. Landes, we've been trying to get hold of you." The nurse fluttered in a most alarming way when she saw her at the front desk.

"Is everything all right?" Christy asked. Her thoughts immediately went to the worst possible scenario. *Something's wrong with the baby. . . .*

"Would you come this way, please?"

Once they were in one of the small examining rooms, the nurse came straight to the point. "Have you gotten your period?"

"No."

The older woman laid a hand on her arm. "I want you to know that we fired her as soon as we found out."

"Found out what?"

"She was a new girl, and she got some of the chart information mixed up. When I gave you the news, she'd put Mrs. Gonzales's information on your chart. Something wasn't right at her examination the next day, and we realized what that girl had done—"

Christy didn't hear anymore. Couldn't.

"I'm so sorry, Mrs. Landes. We tried to call you at home, but that incompetent fool must have copied down the wrong telephone number—"

She'd given them the number of a local Italian restaurant, not wanting them to call her at home.

"I know how badly you wanted this baby. And I hate to be the one to tell you you're not pregnant."

JAKE SIGNED up for acting classes, bought the books the instructor recommended, and set out to find an apartment. He found one, a studio on Laurel in West Hollywood and settled in. After that first agonizing night, he decided he'd tough it out. No more liquor.

He couldn't believe how much he missed her. He'd looked forward to moving to this city for years, and now it just seemed so unreal. Driving to class. Learning the freeways. Shopping for groceries. Hunting for a job. Eating meals he couldn't taste. Lying in bed at night, unable to sleep.

He was thankful he didn't have any friends as yet, no one who knew him and could make any so-called helpful remarks along the lines of what that one distant relative had told him and his sister—*well, you still have each other.* If anyone had dared to say that his and Christy's breakup was for the best, or that an exciting new life was unfolding in front of him, he would have rammed their teeth down their throat.

He'd wanted to be an actor for most of his life, but it didn't mean anything at all without Christy to share it with.

SHE GOT HER PERIOD the next morning. Cried. Couldn't believe her body could hold so much pain. And decided she was going to find Jake and tell him the truth.

She called information. "Jake McCrae. Hollywood."

"I have a J. McCrae in West Hollywood."

"That's him."

She got his answering machine. Heard his voice. "Hi, it's Jake. Leave a message." *Beep.* She couldn't. Some things couldn't be left on tape.

Pete managed to wangle Jake's address out of a female operator, and again offered to drive her to Los Angeles. She declined his help, knowing that if Jake saw them together he would come to some not-so-nice conclusions. She gassed up the Volkswagen, left Boots in Pete's care until she knew what was going on and hit the road just a day later.

Pete had proved to be a good friend. She thought of what he'd said the night before. Pete had no doubt Jake would welcome her back with open arms. "He loves you, Christy. I was always jealous of him, the way the two of you were with each other. A lot of us were. You guys didn't have eyes for anyone else." He scratched Boots beneath his chin as the cat eyed the stale pizza on the coffee table. They were becoming fast friends.

She pushed her little car to its limit, and reached Los Angeles late that morning. She'd bought a map, and found Laurel, the street where Jake lived. It probably wasn't the best thing to just show up, so she tried calling him from a pay phone on Sunset. Once again, she got the machine.

She didn't want to talk to an answering machine, so she parked her VW two apartments down from the one Jake had moved into. His was nice, all pink stucco surrounded by tropical plants. Each apartment seemed to have a balcony, and beyond the iron gate she'd glimpsed the vivid blue of a pool as she'd driven by.

She sat in the car, determined to wait. Before the day was out, she'd talk to him. Beg him to forgive her for her mistake.

She hoped he'd take her back.

"JAKE! Help me with this chair, would you? It's too heavy for me."

Jake was just leaving his apartment for class. He'd had the machine on, he was behind in his reading, but he'd managed to catch up. Richard Bronski's acting workshop was the hardest class he'd ever taken, but it was good for him. There was so much to do, it kept his mind off Christy.

"Please, Jake?" Leanne looked up at him with such a studied expression, her mouth a soft, sexy pout, her eyes calculating. He could picture her practicing in front of the mirror. And he couldn't help contrasting Leanne to Christy's freshness, her beauty. Her innocence.

"Where do you want it?" They started outside, down the walkway toward the security gate.

"You can put it anywhere you want."

Leanne was anything but subtle. He deliberately played it obtuse, not attracted to her in the least. If he'd had to describe her, the first word would have been obvious and the second, coarse. She did nothing for him.

They walked outside the security gate, propped it open. As he turned, she slipped her arm around his waist and smiled up at him.

He was tired, and just wanted to get this whole thing over with. Jake decided it was simply too much trouble to restrain her.

"*Oooh!* Muscles!" Her eyes rounded as she looked up at him. He almost laughed. Did guys really fall for this?

The sooner he dumped her furniture and told her he had to take off for his class, the better. Leanne was a drama queen. She and her boyfriend had spectacular fights; everyone in the apartment complex was aware of their relationship. She regularly came on to other guys to make the masochistic sucker she lived with pay more attention to her.

Hers was one game Jake had no intention of playing. Leanne was simply bad news. A user.

CHRISTY'S HEART started pounding as soon as she saw him, his dark hair, his distinctive walk. He was dressed in jeans and a white T-shirt, and had a book in his hand.

And a woman at his side.

She was dressed in a red sundress that was just a little too tight and low cut. Her heels were high, her lipstick bright, and the way she looked up at Jake, Christy had absolutely no doubts what her plans were.

When she slipped her arm around Jake's waist, something inside Christy twisted. Sharply.

He didn't move away.

The pain was so intense she couldn't breathe. But she could start her car, and she did so, letting the little Bug idle until Jake had carried a large, overstuffed chair inside the security gate, the woman right behind him. Very close.

She put her car in gear and eased out of the parking space. Drove to the freeway totally numb. Got on the entrance ramp and managed to drive almost thirty miles before she was able to take a deep breath.

What did you expect? Jake was a handsome man, and she'd told him to get lost. There was certainly no shortage of beautiful women in a city like Los Angeles. Intelligent women, with the same interests.

But not that woman. She had one thing on her mind, and after the way Christy had treated Jake in the parking lot, how could she blame him for going after her and losing himself in a fun-filled affair?

She wiped her hand across her face, determined not to cry. But the tears came anyway. She'd screwed up her life royally, and had no one else to blame. If she lived to be a hundred, she'd never find a man who meant more to her than Jake. What they had shared came along only once in a lifetime.

Christy stepped on the gas, desperately wanting to get home. And she decided, at that moment, never to come back to Los Angeles.

9

Saturday morning, Memorial Day weekend

SHE WOKE UP knowing that something had changed between them. For the better. Jake slept beside her, on his back, one arm flung over his head. But he wasn't holding on to her, and she liked to think that it might be because he knew she wouldn't run away.

Keith had been right. Meeting Jake's anger with her own would have torn the two of them apart, and their relationship would have been harmed further. Instead she'd refused to enter into it that way, and responded from a deeper place. She'd simply loved him, and it had served to bring them together.

She didn't think he'd still be angry when he woke up.

Christy slid out of bed, grabbed Jake's black T-shirt and slid it over her head. On her, it came to the top of her thighs. She padded downstairs, her feet silent against first the white carpeting then the ceramic tile in the kitchen.

Quietly she set to work, picking up the things Jake had swept off the kitchen table, clearing the other small table by the pool, loading the dishwasher. Once she turned it on, she started to wipe down the gleaming white counters.

Sasha, determined to get some attention, followed her around. Christy stopped as often as possible to pet the little Siamese, but she wanted to finish the cleanup before Jake got up.

She was just handwashing the wineglasses when a noise made her jump.

The small kitchen television. Sasha had walked across the remote and turned it on. Rutger had told her of this habit, and neither of them were sure whether the cat did it on purpose or not.

Now, as she reached for the remote to turn it off, she caught a familiar name. And froze.

"McCrae is being compared to Orson Welles, Kenneth Branaugh and especially Quentin Tarrentino, for the brilliance of his vision, for a film that . . ."

She lowered the sound, watched the brief clip on one of the endless entertainment channels. Rutger had a satellite dish, and managed to get hundreds of stations. She didn't know which one this was, all she knew was that Jake had done a lot better than she'd suspected.

Stupid. You're so stupid. She'd searched for him at the movies, gone to see every one he'd been in. But she wasn't someone who read the credits or even kept up on who the new hot directors were.

And Jake was one of them. At thirty-one, it was more than apparent from this clip that he was about to take the entertainment industry by storm.

Words flashed by, but she barely registered them. Cannes Film Festival... Sundance...brilliant vision...eye of an artist...incredible depth...

And Jake. In a tuxedo, at some event. At a film festival, talking with eager students. Receiving an award, speaking from a podium, flashing the crowd that grin she loved so very much....

A reporter continued with the coverage, excitement tingeing her low, smoky voice. "It's clear that McCrae has quite a career ahead of him, despite persistent rumors that one of the younger actors in his current film is having a bit of trouble with substance abuse—"

She picked up the remote and turned off the set. Then she placed the remote on top of the television, where Sasha couldn't step on it but Rutger could find it when he returned home.

What was Jake up to? Was he going to tell her how wildly he'd succeeded? She thought back to their conversation of the night before.

Do you think I consider myself some big success, because I went to Los Angeles and took a few acting classes? Sure, I've done a lot of movies, and I make a decent living, but do you honestly think I believe I'm a success?

She took a deep breath, struggling to calm the sudden racing of her heart.

...the way she looked at him, the way he was with her—that's success. That's more of a success than any

amount of fame, or any goddamn movie I could have made.

She'd thought he was referring to his acting, but he'd been making reference to the fact that he'd become a director. She didn't watch a whole lot of television, but she'd glanced through the papers each Friday, always looking for his name. The films he'd directed before this one that was now due out had probably been low budget, and might not have even made it out to the desert.

The only person I ever wanted to share that part of my life with was you, Christy. You.

She felt numb inside. Scared all over again. She could feel it starting to come over her, like little tentacles of ice.

Not good enough, never good enough, what if I say or do the wrong thing, he'll realize I won't ever be able to fit into his world....

But Jake didn't put a lot of stock into that world. He wanted a life away from the cameras. He wanted to marry her, start a family, do all the things that, in the end, really mattered.

She would hold on to that thought. It would get her through this weekend with Jake, and she'd see what he wanted to do after that. If he still wanted her to go to Los Angeles with him, she would. She'd try. And if it didn't work—

The thought had her stomach twisted in knots.

She dried her hands and went upstairs to the white bedroom. It was still cool and shaded, the sun had just started to come up. Jake slept deeply, and she wanted him to. That much anger must have been exhausting.

She picked up his jeans and leather jacket, intending to move them to one of the chairs, when a small sketch pad fell out of one of the pockets. She picked it up, walked over and placed the clothing on one of the white, overstuffed chairs, then looked at the sketch pad.

She thought of Jake's mother, and of the talent he'd probably inherited from her. Curiosity overcame her, and she flipped the pad open.

The sketches were really good. They looked like sets, and she realized he was already at work on his next film inside his head, making sketches, visualizing what it would all look like on screen.

She flipped three more pages, but stopped on the fourth. A portrait. The pad itself was only about five by eight inches, so it was small. But he'd captured every detail of her face, even down to the slightly worried expression that always hovered in her eyes.

How well he knows me . . .

She turned a few more pages. Boots. Her father. That one caught her heart, for Jake hadn't captured the despair. He'd remembered the way her father had smiled, that tentative expression, so fleeting. He'd captured it, with pencil, and it tore at her heart.

She slipped the pad back into his jacket pocket, then went silently downstairs. She'd let him sleep as late as he wanted to, and when he got out of bed they'd deal with whatever new set of problems came up. They could get through anything.

She had to believe that. She had to.

THE SUN, high in the clear desert sky, told her it was around eleven. She'd sat out by the pool and done her morning meditation, trying to still her racing mind, trying to get her panic under control. Rationally she knew Jake didn't consider her below him, inferior. But it wasn't Jake's judgment she was fighting.

Afterward, she'd spent some time with the cats. The pool area was enclosed by a high, white stucco wall, so they were allowed to wander outside in that particular area. She took out a brush and groomed all of them, giving extra attention to the temperamental Sasha. The Siamese seemed in a good mood today, and Christy had to smile as she figured out the reason.

Sasha didn't particularly like women. With Jake in the house, she'd curled up next to him every single night, slept close to his head, purring. Christy had snuggled closer to Jake several times during the two nights he'd been here, and every time she'd received a rather baleful look from Sasha as if to say, what do you think you're doing here?

For whatever reason, Rutger's leather sofas were safe.

Once the cats were groomed and left lying out in the sun, dozing, she went back into the kitchen. The wineglasses still needed washing, and she set to work.

Christy had turned on the kitchen stereo, and now recognized John Denver's voice as a song came on. He was singing something about catching the dreamland express.

She smiled, soaping and rinsing the last glass, then running water over her hands. This entire weekend felt like a dream. She'd started it not knowing if she'd ever be able to let go of Jake in her mind, let alone see him in person. Now they were planning a life together.

Christy jumped as she felt hands on her waist.

"Stealing my clothes, are you?" Jake kissed the back of her neck. He was dressed, once again, in his black jeans. Barefoot and shirtless, he was irresistible.

"Jake!"

He'd already eased up the back of the T-shirt, slipped his hands over her bare skin, wrapped his arms around her waist from behind. She was melting fast.

"You should've dragged me out of bed, I would've helped you clean up."

She turned in his arms, her hands still wet, and kissed him—hard.

"Whoa! What's that for?"

"Because I love you."

He cupped her chin in his hands, and the black T-shirt fell back down around her hips. "Are you getting scared? Don't go getting scared on me, Christy."

"Nope," she lied. And she wouldn't get scared. This time nothing would stand in the way of their being together. This time she was going to stifle her fears and make sure everything worked.

"Good." He walked over to the kitchen stereo system, and turned the volume way up. She started laughing as he came back, took her hand, put his other around her waist, started to dance with her in the kitchen, then through the French doors and out toward the pool. "Because today's a fun day, for both of us."

"You're not angry?"

"Waste of time."

She was following his lead, in rhythm to the song on the radio, the easy drum beat, the guitar, the sweet backup harmonies. Now they were out on the tiled area around the pool, in the sunshine, and Jake was whirling her around and around. Music filled the air, and the cats glanced up from their positions on various chairs and chaise lounges, then went back to their sleepy sunning.

She and Jake had always danced well together. It had always felt, to Christy, as if she were coming home. She'd known, way before they'd actually made love, that it would be good. They responded to each other with a language that was purely sensory — looks, touches and even dancing.

She closed her eyes, her head against his shoulder. He'd turned the volume up so loud she was glad Rutger's home was as isolated as it was. But if the sound was carrying over the desert, at least the simple, heartfelt lyrics offered a message of joy.

At that exact moment, she managed to release her fears. What they had was something that transcended a simple explanation. What she knew about filmmaking or any of the rest of Jake's world was immaterial. So she wasn't that sophisticated—she'd learn. He'd teach her. Their love for each other would get them through anything life put in their path.

Jake's breath ruffled her hair as he sang along about rainbows and stars up above. Now the words seemed to have a special meaning, for the two of them alone.

She closed her eyes, swaying her body against his. A perfect moment, bright warm sunshine, his voice, his scent, the touch of his hands . . .

Perfect.

THEY WERE IN the bedroom dressing for dinner when the doorbell rang. She glanced at him.

"Are you expecting anyone?" she asked.

"No. But I think you should answer it."

"Jake!" She was half dressed. He'd informed her at lunch that they were going out to dinner that evening, and now she stood, undecided, in her underwear.

"Would you get it?"

He smiled. "I'm sure it's for you."

"Oh, God." She grabbed her pink silk robe, belted it, then raced barefoot down the stairs, Jake behind her.

The delivery boy was almost obscured behind the huge bouquet of roses.

"You Christy Garrett?"

"Yeah."

"Great. Helluva time finding this place."

She gave him a generous tip. Jake took the massive bouquet, and she started to shut the door.

"Wait!" the delivery boy said. "There's more."

"What?" She couldn't take it all in.

Twelve bouquets in all, each more beautiful than the last. Roses. Daisies. Peonies and lilies, even violets. She knew the florist's name, knew it was one of the most exclusive and expensive flower shops in the desert.

Only the roses had a card.

After the delivery boy left, she simply stared at Jake.

He smiled.

"One for each year, Christy. I wish there had been one for each day." He nodded his head at the small envelope she held in her hand. "Open it."

Her fingers shook, but she did as he asked.

Only rainbows for you from now on. Love, J.

THE TWELVE BOUQUETS made brilliant splashes of vivid color against the pale white walls of Rutger's bedroom.

"Certainly livens up the place," Jake commented, shrugging into his jacket.

"It's a strange bedroom," Christy said. "But maybe he needs all the white to calm him down. He works with so many colors, maybe he just needs a rest from it all when he finally relaxes."

Jake nodded. "Perceptive. I wouldn't have thought of that."

She glowed at his praise. Maybe she hadn't graduated from college, but she had a good mind. And who was to say she couldn't go back to school once they were in Los Angeles? She'd make sure he was proud of her.

She'd make it work.

THE RESTAURANT WAS one of the most romantic in the desert, overlooking the city. The twinkling lights gave Christy the impression that she was floating in a sea of lights. Happiness filled her. She couldn't stop smiling as she and Jake were escorted to their table.

He'd taken care of everything, from the champagne that arrived promptly, to ordering their entire dinner. She was touched beyond words at the thought that he still remembered her favorite foods.

She took another sip of champagne. "You were the one who always remembered. Birthdays. Anniversaries. I can't tell you how much that meant to me."

"I like them. I like those little passages of time, and what those days mean."

She smiled across the table at him. "I still remember that chocolate cake you got me for my seventeenth birthday." She took a deep breath. "The last birthday I celebrated before that was my seventh. My mom—we had a cake with pink frosting and carousel horses. She died right before my eighth birthday, so I didn't expect my dad to do anything. He couldn't. But on my ninth, I remember I waited all day in school, I was so impatient, I knew that when I got home there would be something . . ."

"And there wasn't." He took her hand.

"No. I hinted around a little bit. You know how you think everyone is deliberately forgetting and then they're going to surprise you? That's what I thought."

"How awful."

"I kind of got used to it. I started to realize that if I wanted a birthday, I was going to have to make it for myself. When I turned twelve, I was at the supermarket, shopping, and there was a woman with a box of kittens outside. That's how I got Boots. He was a birthday present to myself."

"You're a survivor, Christy."

"I know." She squeezed his hand. "I want to be able to say this right, Jake. I think that . . . some of the mistakes I made . . . I didn't know what to do because I didn't have anyone to talk to. Except you. And I was so scared of losing you that I kind of . . . clung to you, like you were some kind of lifeboat."

He listened, his dark blue eyes so kind.

"After I met you, it was like . . . you were everything. I didn't have any other friends. So when I found out—when I thought I was pregnant, I—"

"Christy, you don't have to apologize—"

"Yes, I do. I treated you horribly that night. I never thought Pete would hit you, but I knew I had to get you out of town. I thought that if you stayed with me, your life would be ruined."

He squeezed her hand, hard. "There were horrible moments without you. I think the worst thing was just not knowing. I can't tell you how many nights I lay awake, trying to figure out what I'd done—"

Her eyes welled up with tears and she glanced down.

"No, no don't cry, baby. It's in the past. We have the present. We're together, and that's all that matters."

Their dessert was served. Jake had requested that two entire dessert trays were brought to their table— everything the restaurant had to offer.

"You're terrible," she whispered.

"I know how you love sweets."

There were twelve desserts on the trays. She glanced up at him. "Twelve?"

"Coincidence. But a nice one."

She chose the chocolate mousse; he decided on Mud Pie.

"You never had a relationship with Pete, did you?"

His question was deceptively casual, but she could sense the tension behind his words.

"I lived with him, but we were never . . . intimate." She saw no reason to tell him about their short tangle on the couch. It would only hurt him, and she knew Pete would never reveal to anyone what had happened.

"But he was good to you."

"Yeah, he was. He helped me through a rough time, gave me a place to stay." She took a taste of her dessert. "He married a girl out in Riverside. She came into the bar one night and that was it. They have two kids, and they're really happy."

"So he threw off all that biker stuff."

"Right before he started working at the bar."

"I'm glad for him."

"He . . . he told me to go after you. He said you would've been happy about the baby. The bambino, he called it." She couldn't remember those times without that knot coming back to her stomach.

"He was right."

"I did. I drove to L.A. I waited outside the apartment on—Laurel?"

Now he was perfectly still.

"What happened?" he said.

"I saw you with another girl."

"What!"

"You were carrying a chair in for her."

She saw comprehension dawn in his eyes.

"Oh, Lord. Leanne. Christy, she was trouble. She went after anyone in the complex because the guy she lived with didn't pay enough attention to her. She was always coming on to everyone. It was a game to her."

"I thought—she had her arm—"

"Yeah. I know what you saw. I was tired, and that time it was just too much effort to tell her to lay off."

She let go of his hand, set down her spoon, covered her mouth. If that woman hadn't chosen that moment, chosen Jake—

"Don't start doing it, Christy. I know, I did it enough myself. All the what-ifs in the world won't change things. We're here together now, and that's all that matters."

She picked up her spoon again, determined to enjoy the moment.

She wanted to be honest with him. Now was the perfect time to tell him what she'd seen on television that morning, about the way his career seemed to be taking off. She wanted to tell him how proud she was of what he'd done, but how scared she was she couldn't keep up—

"Jake McCrae. Son of a bitch!"

Christy glanced up to see a heavyset fortyish man, balding, deeply tanned, bending over their table, offering his hand to Jake.

"Dan Lowell. We met at Sundance, remember?"

"Yeah."

She couldn't read Jake's expression.

"I saw that clip on 'ET' today. Man, you're about as hot as it's possible to get!" He glanced over at Christy. "And I can see you're taking advantage of it." The smile he gave her went straight to her stomach and twisted it. He was putting her in her place, thinking she was too stupid to see what he was doing.

Jake wasn't. "Dan, this is Christy Garrett, my fiancée."

"Oh. Nice to meet you." His handshake was perfunctory, his attention clearly on Jake. She could have been sitting at another table, for all Dan Lowell cared.

"What have you decided concerning distribution on the next film? I could put you in touch with—"

"Dan. Let me give you a call next week. Right now's not the time."

"Oh." Dan seemed momentarily deflated, as if he couldn't imagine Jake not wanting to talk to him right this minute. "Oh. Okay. Well, call me, okay?"

Jake nodded. Not unkindly. But he was clearly firm in his resolve to not have Dan spoil their evening with business.

"You're a lucky girl," Dan said as he straightened up, preparing to leave. "This guy is the most brilliant director since—hell, I think he's right up there with Kurosawa."

She tried to school her features into a blank expression, but she knew the exact moment when her eyes gave her away. And so did Dan.

"The Japanese director. Have Jake take you to see a couple of his films." He smiled easily, clearly not even realizing how rude he'd been. "We'll talk, Jake."

After Dan left, she glanced back at Jake. His expression was fierce.

"He's a jerk, Christy. Don't let it—"

"I saw the same program, Jake. This morning, in the kitchen. When were you going to tell me?"

He took her hand. "Don't do this."

She squeezed his fingers, feeling as if they were a lifeline. "Can you give me time to catch up?"

"I don't give a damn if you don't know a thing about the industry. It's what I do, but it's not my life. You are."

"But I want to be an asset to you." She swallowed, her throat suddenly tight, aching with suppressed emotion. "I don't want to embarrass you."

"You never have." He kissed her palm. "Do you want to know the first time I saw you?"

She hesitated, knowing he was deliberately changing the subject. A subject they eventually had to discuss. But curiosity overcame her, and she nodded her head.

"I was walking in from the parking lot, and you were running to make a class." His eyes warmed, fairly sparkled. It was obvious he was enjoying the memory. "Your hair was flying out behind you—you knocked me out."

"I noticed you in the cafeteria." She smiled at the memory. "You always sat in the back. I thought you were very handsome, but . . . out of my league."

"Remind me to look Rick up and thank him."

She laughed. "What were you doing at the Circle K that night?"

"I'd heard the two of you were going out. I was driving around, trying to figure out why you'd go out with a guy like him—"

"I wasn't that sharp. I thought he liked me."

"Yeah, he liked you all right. Anyway, I recognized his car out back, and I thought . . . I don't know what I thought. I just wanted to see you."

"How did you—"

"I heard you fighting. I was going in the front to get a Coke, like that was all I was there for, and I heard you yell at him."

She squeezed his fingers. "Thank you. For saving me. Over and over again." She sighed. "Sometimes I think that if I said thank-you to you for the rest of my life, it wouldn't even come close to telling you how I really feel."

"Come back with me. That's good enough for me."

THEY RETURNED to Rutger's dark house. Christy switched on lights, and Jake checked his machine and made a few calls. She was lying in bed petting Sparky when Jake came in.

"I've got to go back to L.A. There's a problem."

"What happened?"

"One of the actors—he's just a kid, actually—has a drug problem."

She knew that, technically, it wasn't Jake's problem. Just as she knew that helping this young man out had nothing to do with his film. It was just the way Jake was.

"Is he in some sort of trouble?"

"He's in jail. He got busted for possession. Cocaine."

"Do you want me to come with you?"

"No. It might be unpleasant."

He'd brought his bag in from his motorcycle, and now was changing clothes, back into the black jeans and T-shirt, into the leather jacket. Now he looked like the Jake who had first taken hold of her arm out by the pool.

Could it have only been two nights ago?

He was ready to go. She followed him down the stairs, out the front door, down the long driveway and past the electronic gate. She saw where he'd parked his bike, hidden behind a huge hibiscus bush.

"I'll come out tomorrow. As soon as I get hold of Keith and ask him if he can house-sit for the remainder of the weekend."

They were at his bike, and she thought Jake was about to get on the powerful machine. Instead he wrapped his arms around her. Held her tight.

"Don't run, Christy."

How well he knew her.

"None of it means a hell of a lot if you aren't there to share it with me."

She wrapped her arms around his waist. Squeezed so hard. Blinked back her tears. She knew she loved him, that had never been in question. At that moment, in his arms, she saw how her fears had driven so much of her life. She was like a little hamster running faster and faster on a wheel. And she had to get off it, in order to have any sort of life with the man she loved.

But she had to give him reassurance now, no matter how she felt inside. And even though the familiar, crippling fears were beginning to entwine themselves around her, like evil snakes. Waiting for her to take a misstep. To fall.

She'd never been able to tell anyone—not even Jake—how frightened she'd been for so much of her life.

The thoughts flashed through her mind with rapid precision. Old territory that had been covered thoroughly, many times before. It was as if her emotions had been caught up in a continual war zone. As far back as she could remember, she'd always been alert, ready for something bad to happen. Never trusting that the good times would last. Always afraid, always hiding what she really felt, not wanting to admit that so much of the time she simply felt overwhelmed.

She'd lived alone, deeply alone, for much of her life, with no siblings, a fading memory of her mother and a defeated, shadow father. And all the time, pretending not to care about what others thought of her when she'd cared so deeply. She just hadn't known how to connect with people.

Loving Jake, opening up to him on so many levels beyond the merely physical, had cost her. Carefully erected walls had come down, brick by painful brick. Her emotional surrender had been complete, and it had been a tremendous effort. She wasn't used to trusting or loving deeply, and she'd given everything she had, and was, over to him.

Now she could feel the fear coming back in waves. Almost assaulting her with its physical force. Drying her mouth, making her stomach clench, her hands shake. *Not good enough, never good enough, he'll see through the facade, he'll realize what an impossible burden you are, what a terrible burden you'll become.....*

Jake was the one shining star in her life. She would do anything, sacrifice anything, even her personal happiness, if it meant not hurting him. She'd done it once before, and she still wasn't completely sure she wouldn't do it again. The fear still threatened to rule her, consume her. Destroy her.

"I'll be there," she whispered in his ear. "I'll come to you. Don't worry about anything, just go help your friend."

She felt that fine tension leave his body. Her reassurance had helped him. She didn't want him traveling back to Los Angeles with any worries about her on his mind.

He laughed then, and she could see he was slightly self-conscious about his vulnerability.

"Besides," she teased. "Even if I didn't, you'd track me down."

"Damn straight."

"I'm stuck with you, Jake McCrae."

"And me with you." He cupped her chin in his hand, looked down into her eyes. "I'd find you."

"I know." She kissed him. "Get going."

He brushed his thumb over her cheekbone. "Hey, you. I'm looking forward to it."

"Me, too."

She watched him drive off into the night. Said a short prayer to ensure his safety. And knew that she had to come to some decisions, make some profound changes, before she could give herself—her *whole* self—back to Jake McCrae.

10

Eleven and a half years ago . . . .

"WE'RE NOT getting anywhere, Pete." Christy poured her roommate another cup of coffee, then set the coffeepot back on the counter.

"There's not a whole lot in here," Pete muttered, picking up the cup without looking at her. She knew he was depressed, and she was getting there. Pete's long, stringy black hair was pulled off his face with a leather thong. He was dressed in faded cutoffs and a navy blue muscle shirt, his attention riveted to the Sunday edition of the paper.

"There's that new bar opening up in Palm Desert. The Castaway. We could try getting jobs there." Christy sat back down at the kitchen table. "The money's got to be better than waitressing." She'd found a job at a nearby Baker's Square, but the minimum wage salary, even with tips, was never going to put her in a position to get ahead.

Pete did seasonal construction work when he wasn't hanging out with his biker friends. But there hadn't been a whole lot of building going on in the desert recently, with the economy limping along. So he was out of work most of the time.

She never mentioned it to him, but Christy knew that her moving in with him had been a godsend. Before she'd found work and brought in a regular paycheck, she'd cleaned the small, one bedroom apartment from top to bottom, then totally rearranged the kitchen so she could cook healthy meals. She'd been scrupulous about cleaning up after Boots, but Pete had never minded living with a cat. He'd fallen in love with the little tabby. And Boots had fallen in love with Pete's regular pizza deliveries — especially pepperoni.

Christy realized, over time, that Pete had essentially lived like a savage. A typical meal had been a take-out pizza and a six-pack before she'd moved in and helped him salvage some of his life. Now the apartment was clean, there was healthy food in the refrigerator, meals were on time and bills were paid.

In return, he'd given her the small bedroom, and a lot of time and privacy. He'd taken up residence on the couch in the living room. Boots, ever the feline diplomat, divided his time sleeping between her small twin bed and the lumpy tan couch.

But Christy wanted more from life.

Jake had been responsible for firing up that little bit of ambition inside her. She'd wanted more than her father had aspired to, more than simply working all day and coming home to fall in front of a television set and tune out. She wanted a job that promised a little advancement, a better paycheck, the opportunity to be with a different group of people.

"Pete?"

"Where is it?"

"Just off the 111, right by that new Ralph's market."

He nodded his head, then folded up the want ads and pushed them to the center of the table. "Aw, what the hell. We can at least go and apply. It can't hurt."

SHE REMEMBERED something she'd learned at a job seminar she'd taken one weekend. To fill out the application as carefully as possible, not leaving any blanks. To think about the answers before she just blithely wrote them down. And to make it as legible and clean as possible.

Pete was muttering as he filled his own out, turning his pencil around and erasing something he'd just written down. She hoped his application was legible.

"Christy Garrett?" A woman from the bar's office in back had come out to the front of the large main room. The Castaway was inside a luxurious resort hotel, the sort of place that would attract people who would be generous—and tip accordingly. Happy vacationers. Hopefully financially well-off vacationers.

"Hi." Christy stood, smoothing her skirt over her hips.

"Right this way."

She didn't know what she'd expected, but it wasn't Keith Tenney. A teddy bear of a man, he practically radiated warmth. She handed him her application and watched his face carefully as he read it over.

"How did you hear about the bar opening up?"

"A friend at work told me."

"So you've waitressed, but haven't done any cocktail waitressing, right?"

"Yes." She took a deep breath, then said, "Actually, I was hoping that I could learn to be a bartender."

He glanced up at her, and there was something she couldn't quite define in his expression. His dark eyes were kind. Assessing. She had a feeling that he was trying to see her—really see her. To go beyond the superficialities, into her character.

"I see."

The silence stretched between them, and she fought her nervousness, determined not to fill it. Then he asked her several other questions, where she was from, where she'd graduated from high school, things like that. She answered them truthfully, with as minimal an amount of information as possible.

"Okay," Keith said.

"Okay?"

"We open in ten days. I'll want you to work a full shift. We'll teach you to bartend as you go, but the pressure won't be bad for the first two weeks, you'll always have a backup. We could try to teach you before we open, but nothing will prepare you for actually working the bar. The policy here is that you can change your schedule as long as you get another bartender to work your hours and clear it with me. You'll wear a Castaway T-shirt and a short black skirt. We'll supply the shirts."

"Thank you."

She was almost to the door—and where she got the nerve to do what she did, she didn't know.

"There's a guy out front—"

"With the hair?"

"Yes. His name is Pete, and...he's a really good guy. I know he doesn't look like much—he might come off a little defensive—but if you'd just give him a chance...." Her voice faded as she saw the expression on Keith's face. "I'm sorry, I shouldn't be telling you how to run your business."

"I was just thinking, Christy Garrett, that if you're as loyal to the people you work for as you are to your friends, we shouldn't have a problem."

She smiled then, a slow smile. And had no idea how it suddenly transformed her face.

"You'll give him a chance?"

"If you'll get him to cut his hair. We need a good bouncer."

"He'd be great."

Keith smiled. "Get out of here and send him in."

THE CASTAWAY proved to be the break both of them had needed. For once in their lives, they had money in the bank and all their bills paid. Christy began to quietly dream again, but none of those dreams ever included a man. She thought of her life in terms of what she would do—alone. Jake had been the only man she'd ever wanted, and if she couldn't have him, she didn't want anyone.

She learned to make drinks. Long Island Iced Teas, Screwdrivers, Vodka Martinis, Gin and Tonics. Daiquiris, Margaritas, Rum and Cokes. Scotch and Sodas. She was a fast learner, and had an instinct as to how to treat a customer. Acknowledge them right away. Make them feel important. Listen to what they wanted to talk about. Offer empathy.

She genuinely liked the clientele, and as a result the tips piled up. She tried to live on her salary and save her tips. Except for the occasional movie or book, there wasn't much she wanted.

Pete seemed happier as well. He flourished at the bar, watching the crowd, keeping things under control, breaking up the occasional dispute well before it could escalate into anything physical. He was a natural, and as Keith gave him more responsibility, Pete blossomed.

They kept the small, one-bedroom apartment. They were conservative financially. They were good friends, and helped each other out. And neither really spoke of the future—they were both too busy surviving the present.

JAKE THREW HIMSELF into his classes, but there was a part of himself he kept distanced. When other students went out in a group after class for coffee, he always excused himself until eventually they stopped asking. That was fine with him. After Christy, he didn't even want to think about another relationship, and he knew that was what would happen if he got too friendly with any of the women in class.

He felt dead, his emotions in a deep freeze. He took the extra reading lists that his teacher, Richard Bronski, provided, and found the books at the numerous used bookstores in Los Angeles, or checked them out of the local library.

There was so much to catch up on, he felt as if he were running in place. He never went anywhere without a book tucked beneath his arm. While waiting in line at the bank or the supermarket, he'd read. Absorb. He was like a sponge, so eager to soak everything up.

So eager to keep thinking so he wouldn't have a chance to feel. Anything.

Almost six months after he'd left the desert he had a bout of what could only be called homesickness. He missed the desert, he missed everything familiar, but he missed Christy most of all. Lying in bed one night in November, he listened to the rain coming down as he thought of phoning Christy.

And wondered at how he could still care.

But he was a man who trusted his emotions, his intuition. And his intuition was telling him to call, to make some sort of contact. Maybe not Christy, but someone who might know what she was up to.

Finally he got up his nerve and dialed Ned, one of the men he'd worked with at the station. They talked of inconsequential things for about ten minutes before Jake asked, with what he hoped was the right amount of casual interest, if his friend had seen Christy.

Ned's hesitation told him all he needed to know.

"I thought you knew. She's living with Pete."

They talked for a few minutes more, Jake desperately pushing down the pain. Once he hung up the phone, he lay back in bed, his hands tucked beneath his head, and stared at the ceiling. He felt absolutely nothing, because he didn't want to allow himself to feel. Couldn't.

After about ten minutes, he picked up a book and started to read.

KEITH TENNEY, her boss, became a combination friend, mentor and inspiration to Christy. He introduced her to things she'd never heard of before. Crystals. Juicing. Vitamins. Meditation. He had a way of simply introducing the strangest concepts into daily conversation and making them sound perfectly natural.

Serenity. Solitude. UFOs. Bee pollen and tofu. Chlorophyll. Acts of kindness. Living with a higher vision.

She soaked it up. Whatever he suggested, she had an open mind. Everything he talked about had a positive effect on her life. And she came to believe that perhaps it wasn't where a person came from, but where they managed to end up that mattered. Keith made her feel as if she could start over again, count for something. Leave all the bad things behind.

But she couldn't leave Jake behind, because he hadn't been part of anything bad.

One day, as she picked up her paycheck, Keith asked her why she never dated. And she surprised herself by opening up to him and telling him the entire story. Not only about Jake, but about her father and the fire. Her fears. Never feeling good enough.

Keith had a way of asking questions, of making one question lead into another in such a way that it was a while before you realized how much you'd told him. It was part of what made him such a phenomenal bartender, on the nights he worked the bar. He believed in doing that, in staying on top of what was really going on in the business. He was in no way a silent partner, isolated in his back office.

Keith simply listened to her that afternoon, and their friendship was solidified. She'd learned that he'd considered a career in psychiatry, but had ended up in business instead, with his brother. Together, the two of them had thought up the concept behind The Castaway. Cast away your cares, come to the club to have a good time.

"You're a survivor, Christy," he'd told her that afternoon. "Don't forget it."

For the first time in her life, as she'd walked out to the parking lot, slid inside her car and simply stared out the window, she believed there might be hope. Maybe not with Jake—with no one else, *no one* if not him—but perhaps she could carve out a life for herself.

SIX MONTHS into his acting class, Jake finally broke down.

He was doing a scene with one of the women in class, a highly emotional, romantic scene. They'd rehearsed all week, discussed motivation, beats, action, everything, and he hadn't seen it coming. But it hit him like a tidal wave.

One of his lines of dialogue, as she walked across the stage, was "Don't leave me."

He got as far as *Don't* before his throat closed. He couldn't speak. Couldn't move. Diane, a dark-haired, petite woman, glanced back at him, the rhythm of the scene off, the dialogue not coming. And to his complete and utter horror, Jake felt the hot tears filling his eyes, the emotion he'd worked so hard at repressing rushing to the surface, threatening to obliterate all of his hard-earned control.

He turned his back to the class, put his hand over his eyes. His shoulders started to shake as he began to weep. The sobs were harsh, painful sounds, wrenched from deep inside.

"We'll take a break now, I think." Richard Bronski's beautiful actor's voice was soft in the large auditorium.

Diane left the stage, the other students filed out into the front, to light up a cigarette or talk, to grab a cup of coffee or tea from the nearby deli around the corner.

Jake couldn't do anything but sob, the feeling coming out in waves. He felt as if he were throwing up his emotions, the physical sensation was that strong.

He didn't even hear Richard come up on stage until the man's arm was around his shoulders and he guided him toward a chair.

Richard was from Eastern Europe, and didn't have the typically phobic North American reaction to a man offering another comfort by simply touching him. Even when Jake sat down, his teacher kept a hand on his shoulder, offering simple human empathy. Jake hadn't let anyone close to him for a long time, and now knew that hand was a lifeline.

"So that scene brought something up, I think." Richard's voice was quiet. Concerned.

Jake could only nod.

"A woman, of course."

Jake nodded again.

Richard lit one of his French cigarettes, offered Jake one. He shook his head. Usually it was forbidden to smoke inside the theater, but for some reason Richard was making an exception.

"How do you feel?" he asked, once Jake had stopped crying. He'd handed him some tissues from the bathroom, and now Jake blew his nose, wiped his red eyes. And felt such shame.

"Ashamed."

"Why?"

"Because—" He gestured helplessly around the theater, trying to indicate where the rest of the students usually sat.

"Because they saw you break down?"

Jake nodded.

"You think none of them has ever cried like that?"

Jake didn't know what to say. He knew no one would come back into the theater until Richard was through, so they had some time to sort this out.

"The hardest thing in the world, for me, as a teacher," Richard said conversationally, as if he hadn't just seen Jake sobbing his guts out, "is to get a woman angry or a man to cry. We live in a sick culture, where it is somehow a good thing, a respected thing, not to express one's emotions."

Jake said nothing, not really knowing where this was heading. At this point, not really caring.

"You remember Aristotle?"

Only Richard Bronski could bring Aristotle into a conversation at the drop of a hat, as if he were one of his elderly relatives who he enjoyed talking about.

Jake nodded.

"The whole concept of catharsis?"

Jake nodded again.

"That was what happened. The words, the feelings, brought up the emotions." Richard blew out a thin plume of smoke, then squinted his sharp, blue-gray eyes against the haze. He ran his hands through his thick, silvery hair.

"I was out of control."

"As an actor, yes. As a human being, no."

"But—"

"This is a class, Jake. A place to learn. A safe place."

"But I shouldn't have—"

Richard moved his large hand from Jake's shoulder, covered one of Jake's hands with his own.

"Let me tell you what I saw. I saw a young man struggling to achieve mastery over deep emotion he's been suppressing for the six months I've taught him. Sorrow. Grief. Anger." He took another drag of the French cigarette, then let the smoke out, softly, through his nose. "You bottle all that up, it will kill you in the end."

Jake had no answer for that.

"You know what else I saw? Two women started to cry. One was sitting next to me. You affected them. You think they don't know, the way you keep to yourself? They all respect that, but sooner or later you have to rejoin. You have to keep going."

"Ah, God..." Jake put his head in his hands, wiped his eyes.

"You loved her."

He nodded, his eyes still covered.

"She left you."

He nodded again.

Richard sat back in his seat, and Jake could hear the wood creak. "Don't leave me," Richard said softly. "Three words. Powerful words. Powerful emotions."

Jake looked up as his teacher stubbed out his cigarette.

"Don't be ashamed to feel, Jake. The great ones, the actors, the writers, the painters, that's what they do. A great service to society. They bring us back to our feelings. And you cannot give that to people unless you understand your own." He smiled. "So, yes, on one level you were out of control as an actor and the scene was interrupted. Not finished. But on another level, it was a great success."

Jake managed a shaky smile.

Richard sat forward in his chair, looked at his student intently. "You're safe here, Jake. I want you to know that, and to be able to do your best work. No one will think less of you because of what happened tonight."

THAT NIGHT, other emotions surfaced and Jake dreamed about Christy. Erotic, sensual dreams. Dreams in which he made love to her until she surrendered, left the desert, came back to the city with him. Dreams that made him wake up covered with sweat, muscles taut, sexually aroused.

And even though he shook with the force of his emotions, he had to admit it was better than being one of the walking dead. The body didn't lie. What he'd tried to force down had come to the surface with a vengeance.

He wouldn't deny his feelings any longer.

THE YEARS WENT BY, for both of them.

Christy worked at The Castaway and eventually started Mom Cat. Her business flourished, and she had a healthy bank balance. Pete married and moved on. She bought a condo, furnished it the way she liked it. Felt safe—but dead inside. She had two disastrous sensual encounters, and began to think about security. Arthur Beck walked into the bar one night, and she knew she'd found that security if she wanted it.

Keith simply looked on.

Jake continued his classes. One evening, Richard offered him a job. He was going to Poland to direct a film; he and his wife would be out of the country for six months. Would Jake like to learn, firsthand, what directing was about? Richard needed a smart, sharp assistant. Jake didn't hesitate, even for a heartbeat.

Europe changed his life. He bought art supplies, began to sketch, see things in a different way. Found that he loved directing more than acting. Richard laughed when he told him that, said he'd suspected it all along. Jake worked so hard he fell asleep exhausted each night, but woke in the mornings ready to get back to the set. He was working to full capacity—this was what he'd dreamed of.

He could almost make himself forget Christy.

He found that he went after brunettes, because he didn't want to mistake any other woman for her. None of them came close. He simply had to close his eyes and he could see her. Remember. He sketched her, thought of her, wished she could have seen all of this with him.

He assisted Richard on three movies and acted in four more before he directed a low budget film of his own. Amazingly it made money. The studios took notice, gave him a slightly bigger budget the next time. He came in on time and under budget. Then he did it again. The entertainment world sat up and took notice. Jake worked like a demon, but he never forgot her.

And almost twelve years to the day that she'd left him, he got on his motorcycle and went back to the desert, determined to find the truth.

11

Sunday morning, Memorial Day weekend

SHE WAS UP ALL NIGHT, cleaning Rutger's house, obliterating all traces of either her or Jake. Leaving it just the way she'd found it. Changing the bedsheets, laundering the towels. Washing the last few dishes. She'd take Keith the keys, ask him to watch the house and care for the cats for a few days. He'd do it for her, once she explained the circumstances.

And the entire time, as she worked, she willed herself to be unafraid. She wanted to believe she and Jake had a future together. If love counted for anything, they did. Then why did she still have such doubts? As Christy scrubbed and polished the house, cleaned the litter boxes, stacked the mail, she knew that self-doubt had been a crushing presence in her entire life. Now she had a chance to get beyond it all, and she desperately wanted to take it.

Logically she knew this.

Emotionally she was afraid.

She arrived at Keith's house around noon. The party was winding down. A few stragglers were sprawled on the couch or asleep in other rooms. Keith himself was standing out on his huge redwood deck, watching the bright sunlight and clouded shade play over the mountains.

She sat down on a chaise lounge, not wanting to disturb him. But he sensed her presence immediately.

"Christy." He turned and smiled.

Keith had, over the last decade, changed her more than anyone else. Showed her new possibilities. She loved him like the brother she'd never had, and would always consider him part of her family. Now, as he came toward her, she knew he was studying her, seeing subtle differences most people probably wouldn't notice.

But Keith looked deep.

"What's up?" He sat down next to her. They were as good as alone; the house was quiet except for a few lingering party people.

Briefly she told him what had happened since she'd left the bar on Thursday night. Her swim. Jake wanting revenge. Their time together, their anger and arguments and the way they'd loved each other. Jake needing the truth, their uncovering of the past. And his determination that they could still have a life together.

The past two days had been exhausting. The best two days of her life.

She told him what she planned to do, then asked him if he could watch Rutger's house. Of course he agreed, and she gave him the keys. But he saw more than she cared to reveal, and with a flash of insight

Christy realized that was exactly why she'd come to him. She needed kindness, compassion and insight.

"Why don't you think it's going to work?"

She couldn't meet his eyes.

"I guess . . . because . . . Keith, he's going to be a world-class director, he's going to take on the *world*, and I didn't think I was good enough for him when I was in high school."

He took her hand. "Little girl, I'm going to have to be tough with you, but I hope you'll take what I say in the spirit it's given."

She met his eyes. "Help me, Keith."

"It's ego, Christy. You're operating from your ego, and every time any of us does that, we're as good as dead."

"Love and fear," she whispered. "You know, I thought of that one night with Jake. He was so angry, and I remembered that talk we had at the bar. And I knew he was afraid."

"You got it. And now you're letting that fear get the better of you. And how the old ego loves that. Christy," he said, taking her face in his hands, "I love you like a sister. I've watched you get on with your life, but it was always as if a piece was missing. Some vital little spark wasn't quite there. That glow."

She knew exactly what he meant.

"And it wasn't there with old Arthur." He grinned, then dropped his hands. "At least I don't have to talk you out of that decision."

"No. I'll meet Arthur for lunch next week and tell him I can't marry him. I owe him that much."

"I don't think you'll hurt him, Christy. He'll just look around for someone else to marry. No offense meant."

"None taken."

"Good. But what I wanted to tell you—the minute I glanced around and saw you...you're different. I've never seen you look the way you look now. Softer. Glowing. Even through the fear. If you hadn't said a word to me about Jake, I still would've known something had changed you. Profoundly."

She was silent, taking this all in.

"And I'll bet things changed for him, as well."

She nodded her head.

"Neither of us could get on with our lives, Keith. It was as if . . . we were waiting for each other."

"And he finally had the courage to come all the way out here and find you. Try to either put it to rest and move on, or see if something could be salvaged from what the two of you once shared. He's a good man. I hope to meet him someday."

"You will." She was already feeling better. Just being with Keith sometimes did that to her, he was such a strong presence. He always soothed her, and knew the right thing to say. He helped her see her life in a different way, gave her hope. Keith always worked for the greater good.

She listened carefully.

"It's a basic truth, Christy. All the great philosophies say it, in different ways. It's the little self fighting the big Self. The ego separates, and always causes us a great deal of pain. Love, if you let it work through you, brings us all together. Heals. It's the greatest force there is." He grimaced. "I probably sound like that Kung Fu guy, what was his name?"

"Kane."

They both laughed, remembering the afternoon they'd rented *Pulp Fiction*.

"I will walk the earth, like Kane in Kung Fu," Keith said, then laughed again.

"Don't ever feel that way about what you say. It always makes sense. To me, at least."

Keith smiled. "Ah yes, Grasshopper. You have learned well." His expression sobered. "Just think about this. You're ready to die. To move on. What would you regret most?"

She already knew the answer. "Not going to him. Not giving this a chance."

"You have more than a chance, Christy. You know you do." He took her hand, linked his fingers through hers. "So. The path is right there, and you know where you're going."

She nodded, then yawned.

"You didn't sleep all night."

"Yeah."

"Lie down for a few hours. He probably won't even be home until this evening, what with getting that kid out of jail. I'll wake you up in time to drive in."

"Thanks, honeybear." She lay down on the soft chaise, and Keith brought a light blanket and placed it over her. The lounge chair was in the shade, so she wouldn't burn.

She was drifting off to sleep as she heard Keith's voice one last time. "Little Grasshopper, the road to enlightenment is long and difficult. So you should always bring snacks and a magazine."

She fell asleep with a smile on her lips.

THE DRIVE WAS EASY, so many people were taking Monday off as well. Traffic was light, and Christy pushed the Thunderbird to its limit, all the time remembering another drive she'd taken, so long ago.

Keith's words stayed in her mind, and she found that if she focused on the love she and Jake shared, there was no room for the fear. Oh, she had no illusions that it wouldn't rear its ugly little head again in her life, at dark moments. But she would do her best to try to let more light into her life, to chase out the darkness.

Beginning with loving Jake.

The San Bernardino Freeway merged with the Hollywood Freeway, and then she was exiting onto Gower Street. Jake had written out directions for her, and she followed them to the letter. Up Beachwood, toward the hills. Past the little square with a small market and coffee shop. To the right, then left up another winding street.

And then she was there.

The house was huge, stucco, old-fashioned. Built in the thirties or forties, when Hollywood was in its glory days. She parked her car in the driveway, then walked slowly up the brick walk. Unlocked the door with the key Jake had given her. Walked inside, locked the door behind her.

The house was cool and silent. She hadn't seen Jake's car outside...perhaps he wasn't home yet. She wandered down the hallway, past rooms that weren't quite furnished. And she realized Jake needed someone to help him make this house a home. Someone to attend to their lives, to the real living that went on between jobs. Someone to watch over their happiness.

She could do that. She'd let it go once, and it had been the most painful and profound lesson she'd ever learned. Now she was being given a chance at happiness again, and knew it for the gift it was.

She headed toward the end of the hallway, then down some stairs. Toward light. There was a room at the end. It had to have a lot of windows because it was brightly lit with sunshine. She was drawn toward it, walking silently over the carpeted hallway.

Christy had barely reached the doorway when she realized Jake was in the room. She stopped, stepping back, not wanting him to see her yet. Wanting to have a chance to watch him, knowing he was back in her life if she had the courage to take that last step.

The room was filled with rainbows.

It was an old-fashioned sunroom, spacious with lots of windows facing the sunset. Light filled the high ceilinged room, light that illuminated and suffused the painting on the walls. Rainbows. All over. Every shade, every color, so beautifully realized that it took her breath away... She could only stand and stare.

And Jake. His back was to her as he took a break from painting, but she saw the slight slump of his shoulders, the way he held his body. Tightly, as if in anticipation of pain. It was a private moment, one she was sure he would never have let her see had he known she was there.

He's just as scared as I am.

She knew, in that instant, he didn't expect her to come. She and Jake were more alike than not, both of them expecting the worst. Their past had conditioned them to it, but now she had a chance for a new future, filled with happiness. One she could create with Jake.

She'd remember this moment forever, a moment in time in which she was being given a chance to begin again. A moment as powerful as the one in which Jake had pulled her out of that car and offered her the shirt off his back.

"Hey," she called softly.

He turned, the brush in his hand. He wore only a pair of faded jeans, and there were little specks of colored paint high on his shoulders. She watched as he ran his fingers through his hair. Fingers that shook. Oh, she wouldn't have noticed if she hadn't really been looking.

Keith had taught her that. To look deeply.

"Hey, yourself." He set the brush down on a square of newspaper, then stood there.

And she realized what he wanted. Needed from her. He'd traveled over a hundred miles to the desert to find her, but billions of miles, across the stars, emotionally. Now she sensed he needed her to cross the room to him, to leave him in no doubt that she would never walk out on him again.

Love or fear, Christy. Take your pick.

She started that walk, across that sunlit room, and the thought flitted through her mind that perhaps if she'd never lost Jake for those twelve years, she'd never have been aware of what she'd had, of how they'd been blessed. And she remembered something Keith had once said about diamonds, about how they were created through the most intense pressure. But once created, they were one of the strongest substances on earth.

She'd come through the fire. So had he. Now their life together, the life she'd been waiting for, was about to begin.

She took those final steps, felt his strong, familiar arms close around her. His chin came to rest on the top of her head and Christy closed her eyes, slowly letting out the tense breath she'd been holding.

She was home.

HE CONCENTRATED on painting rainbows, wondering the entire time if Christy would be in his house before dark.

Sunset was fast approaching. Normally he loved this time of day, but now his stomach was churning, his hands shaking. She did this to him, as surely as she brought out the most passionate side of his nature. He loved her, but he hated this feeling of being out of control.

Here, painting, he could pretend he had some semblance of control.

He'd gotten Nick out of jail. The young actor had been apologetic, but wary. Defensive. Jake had taken him to a nearby coffee shop, offered him a lifeline much like the one Richard Bronski had given him so many years ago. He still wasn't sure Nick was going to take it, but he'd made sure the actor had known it was there.

Then he'd come home to wait. Hadn't been able to stand the tension. Picked up his brushes and retired to the sunroom. And all he could think about was sitting here with Christy, watching sunsets.

"Hey."

He turned at the sound of her voice. She was standing in the doorway, wearing jeans and a pink sleeveless top, and she'd never looked more beautiful to him.

He ran his fingers through his hair. Fingers that shook. He hoped she didn't notice how nervous he was, then realized he didn't care. He didn't want any more secrets from her, ever again. It didn't matter if he was out of control for the rest of his life, as long as she was by his side.

"Hey, yourself." He set his brush down on a square of newspaper, then waited. Couldn't have moved if his life depended on it. Wanted her to come to him so desperately. Knew that if he took those few steps, he'd never know if he made the decision for her.

I came all the way out to the desert for you. Please walk across the room to me, Christy. Please reassure me and let me know you want this as much as I do....

Then she started toward him, came to him, and he wrapped his arms around her, tucked her head beneath his chin, held her as tightly as it was possible to hold another human being. And all the pain, all the hurt and rage and sorrow was worth it, just to get to this moment in time.

He was home.

He found his legs were shaky with emotion, and he slowly sat down, taking her with him, his back against a part of the painted wall that had dried several days ago. He maneuvered them so she was sitting in his lap, and it was enough, being this close, for several minutes. Neither of them said a thing, both so glad to be together at last.

"Come with me," Jake said quietly, getting to his feet, helping her to her own. She followed him to the upstairs master bedroom, and he knew from the expression on her face that she thought he wanted to make love.

"No, wait." He went into the large, walk-in closet, to the dresser inside, to the top drawer. He wished, at that moment, that he would have had everything ready, orchestrated one of those perfect Kodak moments. But he knew he couldn't wait, had to claim her as his own. Had to do it now.

He sat next to her on the king-size bed and handed her the small jewelers box. She simply stared at it, then looked up at him.

"Open it, it's not going to bite you." Now he was impatient, he wanted her to see how much she meant to him. How every bit of his success had been for her.

The large diamond sparkled brilliantly in the evening light. He heard her soft gasp, smiled as she took the ring out of the satin-lined box and admired it. Then she almost reduced him to tears, drawing hold of the slender gold chain around her neck. She pulled it out of the neckline of her top, and he saw both his class ring and the tiny chip of diamond in the promise ring he'd given her over a decade ago. The one she'd thrown away.

She'd obviously gone back and found it. Even then, when she'd been determined to drive him away, it had meant something to her. The thought filled him with a deep, primal joy.

He tried to make light of his emotions.

"I told you I'd get you a better one. So it took me twelve years, but I did it—"

Then her arms were around his neck, holding him close, her body quivering with emotion. He knew she still held the diamond ring in her fist, but now Christy was pulling him down on the bed with her, kissing his face. It wasn't a prelude to lovemaking, it was deeper than that. More tender.

"Jake," she said quietly. "I'll never leave you again."

He hadn't known, until she said the words, how desperately he'd needed to hear them. He took the ring from her closed fist, and slipped it on her finger where it belonged.

"I may get scared once in a while, or think I'm not good enough for you." She smiled up at him and he smoothed a strand of her pale blond hair off her cheek. "But all you have to do is tell me to check the old ego at the door."

He laughed. Something had changed in her. In both of them. This time, he had no doubts they were going to make it.

This time, when they made love, it was without heat or haste, but filled with emotion. Closeness. A rediscovering of the deepest parts of each other.

Just before he drifted off to sleep, his arms around her, Jake felt Christy's hand against his cheek, softly stroking his face. He opened his eyes.

"Thank you for coming after me."

He took her hand. Kissed it. "I didn't do it with the most noble intentions. I was out for revenge."

She smiled. "It didn't last long."

"No. It couldn't, with you."

He felt the fine tension in her body, knew there was something else. Waited.

"Jake?"

"Hmm?"

"Will you do me a favor?"

"Anything."

"Will you forgive me?"

He didn't even hesitate. "Baby, there's nothing to forgive."

Her eyes filled as she looked up at him.

"Oh, Jake."

"It's true. It's in the past." And as he said it, he felt the last vestiges of anger, fear, pain, leave him. It was as simple as that, simply all in the way you looked at the world.

"Forgive me?" he whispered. He kissed her lips, then the soft pulse point at the base of her throat.

"There's nothing to forgive. There never was." Her voice sounded tight with emotion.

He kissed her again, long, lazy kisses that drove both of them crazy. He slid between her thighs, positioned himself for that ultimate joining, looked down at her face, dreamy and flushed with arousal. Watched as he entered her, body and soul, their union complete.

Jake McCrae was finally at peace.

This month's
irresistible novels from

LOVE ME, LOVE MY BED by Rita Clay Estrada

The Wrong Bed

Beth McGruder's fantasy bed was everything she'd imagined, except it arrived with something extra by mistake. In her spare room she now had a king-size monstrosity she was dying to get rid of. And in her own room she had the gorgeous owner, Duke McGregor, who was anxious to take possession...

NOBODY'S HERO by Patricia Keelyn

Rebels and Rogues

Private investigator Sam Cooper only took on cases that he couldn't get involved with emotionally. He didn't need any romantic entanglements making the job tougher. But then sexy Jessie Burkett came to him for help. Too late Sam realized that he'd like to become involved with *her*, intimately...

THE LAST SEDUCTION by Elda Minger

Jake McCrae had never got ex-sweetheart Christy Garrett out of his system. Time *hadn't* healed his wounded heart. Now he was back in Palm Springs. Determined to find answers and uncover her secrets. Determined to make slow, agonizing, passionate love to Christy just once—and then leave. For good.

A VALENTINE WISH by Gina Wilkins

Dean Gates didn't believe in love...or in ghosts. When he bought the historic Cameron Inn, Dean encountered both. The gorgeous, if rather ethereal, Mary Anna Cameron wanted Dean to uncover the mystery surrounding her demise. But all Dean wanted was to have Mary Anna haunt him indefinitely...

Spoil yourself next month
with these four novels from

AN INCONVENIENT PASSION by Debra Carroll

Joanna Clooney was forced to ask her ex-husband, Reid, to
pretend they were still married to help her mother to recover
from a life-threatening illness. But their marriage of convenience
turned into an impossible sexually-charged charade as they
fought their attraction. There was only one place it could end—
in bed!

CALL ME by Alison Kent

It wasn't Harley Golden's style to call a perfect stranger and
have phone sex. But after one brief encounter with the
unforgettable Gardner Barnes, she was doing all sorts of
impulsive, adventurous things—like flying to see him, falling in
love, getting pregnant...

WICKED WAYS by Kate Hoffmann

Innkeeper Hallie Tyler's life is in chaos. The inn is filled to
capacity, thanks to her two imaginative aunts' decision to
resurrect—and embellish—an old family legend. Now she's
overrun with vampire chasers. But what's worse, Hallie finds
herself falling for the sexy, enigmatic Tristan Montgomery...who
seems to show an unusual interest in her neck...

THE OUTLAW

Rogues

Wolfe Longwalker is about to be lynched for a crime he didn't
commit. Until Noel Giraudeau, a modern-day princess, finds
herself in 1896 Arizona, rescuing him. On the run from the law,
their passionate adventure quickly turns into something much
more real...but Noel's destiny is back in her own time.

MILLS & BOON®

Four remarkable family reunions,
Four fabulous new romances—

Happy Mother's Day

Don't miss our exciting Mother's Day Gift Pack
celebrating the joys of motherhood with love, laughter
and lots of surprises.

SECOND-TIME BRIDE	Lynne Graham
INSTANT FATHER	Lucy Gordon
A NATURAL MOTHER	Cathy Williams
YESTERDAY'S BRIDE	Alison Kelly

Special Promotional Price of £6.30—
4 books for the price of 3

Available: February 1997

New York Times bestselling author

JAYNE ANN KRENTZ

Legacy

A story of two unlikely lovers

Honor Mayfield thought that her chance
meeting with Conn Landry was a stroke of
luck. Too late she realised she was falling for
someone who was seeking to avenge a legacy
of murder and betrayal.

"A master of the genre...nobody does it better!"
—Romantic Times

**AVAILABLE IN PAPERBACK
FROM FEBRUARY 1997**